The Voices of the Pioneers

The Voices of the Pioneers:
Homeschooling in Minnesota

Given Hoffman & Eileen Hoffman

authorHOUSE®

AuthorHouse™ LLC
1663 Liberty Drive
Bloomington, IN 47403
www.authorhouse.com
Phone: 1-800-839-8640

Published by AuthorHouse 02/27/2014

ISBN: 978-1-4918-6889-8 (sc)
ISBN: 978-1-4918-6888-1 (hc)
ISBN: 978-1-4918-6887-4 (e)

Library of Congress Control Number: 2014903611

Scripture taken from the New King James Version®. Copyright © 1982 by Thomas Nelson, Inc. Used by permission. All rights reserved.

Any people depicted in stock imagery provided by Thinkstock are models, and such images are being used for illustrative purposes only. Certain stock imagery © Thinkstock.

This book is printed on acid-free paper.

Contents

To our Lord and Savior, Jesus,
Who orchestrated all of these meetings and miracles
to accomplish something close to His heart:
parents teaching their children about Him.

And to all the wonderful support group leaders
and volunteers who give of themselves to
encourage and bless others.

Deuteronomy 11:19
"You shall teach them [God's words] to your
children, speaking of them when you sit in your house,
when you walk by the way, when you lie down,
and when you rise up."

Acknowledgments

First and foremost, I would like to give credit for this book to Linda Watkins. She was the one who approached me and asked me to do a history project for MÂCHÉ's 30th Anniversary.

I want to give special thanks to my mother for being willing to create this book with me. Without her this project never would have come to fruition. I also would like to thank my family, especially my father for putting up with our crazy writing hours, my sister BriAnn for helping with editing, and my brother-in-law Mark for rubbing out our knotted shoulders and bringing us chocolate.

My deepest gratitude to everyone who contributed to this book:

Personal oral interviews:
Jim and Pam Coleman
John and Lynne Cooke
Michael Donnelly
Kathryn Duerst
Bonnie and Erin Erpelding
Michael Farris
DuWayne and Miriam Heppner
Dean and Ruth Lindstrom
Jerry and Linda McMillin
Bob Newhouse
Jeanne Newstrom
Gen Olson
Roger and Merryl Schurke
John Tuma
David and Linda Watkins

Written submissions:
Carl and Carla Biederman
Brad and Nancy Bjorkman
Mac and Karen Bryant
Karl and Suzanne Solum
Maren Stowman
Jerry and Pam von Gohren
John and Doris Wetjen

Those who provided pictures:
Colemans
Cookes
MÂCHÉ
McMillins
Marianos
David J. Oakes

Our editors:
BriAnn Beck
Tracie Henkel
Doris Wetjen
Kate Ophoven (for the legal citations)

Unit Study:
BriAnn Beck

My heartfelt thanks to AuthorHouse's staff for making this book a reality.

Introduction

When Linda Watkins approached us about this project in September 2012, I was intrigued by the idea. Even as a homeschool graduate, I knew very little about the history of homeschooling. Basically, I knew homeschooling had not always been legal in Minnesota, and that was about it.

When my mom (Eileen), Linda, and I talked about the project, none of us was really sure what it would look like in the end. We knew it would involve personal interviews with people who were there, who helped fight to make homeschooling legal in Minnesota, but would it be a pamphlet with quotes, a summarization of the interviews, a compilation, a history book, or what?

After hearing just the first couple of interviews, I knew summarizing the interviews would not do them justice. So we chose instead to make this book a compilation of primary source history.

In December 2012, we sat down with John Tuma, who shared with us some of the events significant to the history of homeschooling. At this meeting, John handed me the court case *State v. Newstrom* and pointed out that it said Jeanne Newstrom lived in a little town close to where we lived. I wondered what the likelihood was that she was still in our area. Once home, I pulled out our local phone book. Sure enough there was a Jeanne Newstrom listed, but was it the right Jeanne Newstrom? I dialed the number and held my breath. A woman answered, and I said, "Hi, is this Jeanne Newstrom?" She said, "Yes." I hurriedly asked, "Were you involved in a Minnesota Supreme Court case in 1985?" "Yes." Thrilled, I asked her if she would be interested in allowing us to interview her for this project.

In January 2013, we met with Jeanne Newstrom, who shared with us her story about the court case that helped make homeschooling legal.

Over the next twelve months, we drove around Minnesota, talking to people and gathering their stories. We made a brief side trip while out at a conference in Colorado to meet with the Colemans, and, at another conference in Washington, D.C., we had the opportunity to talk with Michael Farris and Michael Donnelly.

As a result, this book is a collection of over twenty different people's stories involving homeschooling in Minnesota. We hope you enjoy reading these accounts as much as we enjoyed hearing them.

To homeschool parents or teachers: If you are interested in using this book as a curriculum, please consult the unit study guide provided at the back of this book.

Timeline of Minnesota Homeschool Education

Significant references are bolded and italicized names i.e. (*Newstrom*) reference the person who discusses that information.

1885

The first compulsory education law in Minnesota
"An Act Requiring the Education of all Healthy Children"
This law is the foundation of all compulsory education laws in Minnesota, including the law that is eventually formed by the Compulsory Attendance Task Force.
(See Appendix A, I.)

1925

June 1, 1925 - ***Pierce v. Society of Sisters***
Parents gain the right to choose to put their children in public or private schools with the Pierce v. Society of Sisters decision delivered by Justice McReynolds of the U.S. Supreme Court.
(See Appendix A, II.)

July 21, 1925 - Scopes "Monkey" Trial
Evolution begins to be taught in the public schools.
(See Appendix A, III.)

1962-1963

Prayer and Bible reading are taken out of the public schools; Christian school enrollment increases dramatically.
(See Appendix A, IV.)

1964

John Holt writes *How Children Fail*.

After conducting research to promote reform in the public schools, he concludes that homeschooling is a superior option. (*Newstrom*)

1972

May 15, 1972 - *Wisconsin v. Yoder*

The U.S. Supreme Court decides the Yoder family's decision to homeschool their children falls under their First Amendment right to religious freedom.

This becomes a useful precedent for many other court decisions on homeschooling in the United States.

(See Appendix A, V.)

1975

Dr. Raymond and Dorothy Moore write *Better Late Than Early.* They explain that early formal education of children can damage their desire to learn, and waiting to start formal education can be an advantage.

The Moores are considered the grandparents of the modern homeschool movement; they have also written *Home Spun Schools*, *Home Style Teaching*, *Home Grown Kids*, *Home Built Discipline*, and *School Can Wait II* (the scholarly version of *Better Late Than Early*).

(*Newstrom, Duerst, McMillin*)

1976

John Holt writes *Instead of Education.*

He advocates self-directed learning and useful jobs to develop healthy character in children.

(*Newstrom*)

1977

John Holt publishes *Growing Without Schooling* magazine.

The publication provides encouragement for the growing homeschool movement.

Jerry and Pam von Gohren begin home educating.

1979

Dr. James Dobson interviews **Dr. Raymond Moore on "Focus on the Family" radio program**, introducing American parents to the idea of homeschooling.
(See Appendix B, I.)
(*Coleman, McMillin, Wetjen*)

Dr. Raymond Moore speaks on the Phil Donahue Show.
(*Lindstrom*)

1980

The Colemans begin homeschooling.

The Schurkes begin homeschooling.

Jeanne Newstrom begins home-based education with her children in the afternoons.

Teaching Home magazine is founded by Pat and Sue Welch. The publication provides inspiration for the homeschool movement.
(*McMillin*)

1981

January - The Colemans are reported for not having their children in public school.

August - Jeanne Newstrom is informed by Superintendent Maertens that she must return her children to public school full-time.
(See Appendix A, VII.)

1982

Gen Olson is elected to the Minnesota Senate.

Roger Schurke discusses homeschooling liberty with Michael Farris while working with him in Washington State.
(*Schurke, Farris*)

Karl and Suzanne Solum begin homeschooling.

Ruth Lindstrom becomes more convicted about homeschooling and goes to meet the Coleman family and observe their homeschool.

August and September - Donald and Kathleen Budke go to court to ensure their right to the free exercise of their religious convictions to teach and disciple their children at home. They lose in Otter Tail County Court and file an appeal. The Budkes contact attorney John Eidsmoe for help with their case.
(See Appendix A, VI.)
(*Schurke, Newstrom*)

October - Superintendent Maertens requests Jeanne Newstrom be charged with a misdemeanor for violating the Compulsory Attendance Law.
(See Appendix A, VII.)

Minnesota Homeschoolers' Alliance (MHA) is founded.
(*Facebook.com. About*)

1983

The National Commission on Excellence (NCE) presents their two-year study on the public schools in a report titled "A Nation at Risk: The Imperative for Educational Reform."
(See Appendix B, II.)

Jeanne Newstrom receives a summons to court.
(*Newstrom*)

The Lindstroms begin homeschooling and form Rochester Area Association of Christian Home Educators (RAACHE).

Michael Farris and Michael Smith form the **Home School Legal Defense Association** (HSLDA).
(*Schurke, Farris*)

Fall - Roger and Merryl Schurke and Jim and Pam Coleman meet and **begin to pray** about forming a homeschool organization with Christian leadership in Minnesota.
(See Appendix B, III.)

November - **The organizational meeting for MÂCHÉ** (Minnesota Association of Christian Home Educators) is held in the **Powderhorn Park** building in south Minneapolis with approximately fifty people in attendance.
(See Appendix B, III.)
(*Coleman, Schurke, Newhouse*)

The Seventh District Court of Otter Tail County reverses an earlier decision and grants the Budkes the freedom to homeschool on the basis of their First Amendment rights.
(See Appendix A, VI.)

Robert Newhouse founds Teaching Effective Academics and Character at Home (TEACH).

1984
The **first MÂCHÉ newsletter** is sent to member families.

January, April, and September - MÂCHÉ holds workshops around the state, as well as a picnic in June. The April meeting is held at Grace Church of Edina, with over 360 attendees.
(*Coleman*)

Robert and Bethany Newhouse join the MÂCHÉ board of directors.

The Cookes begin to homeschool.

The Biedermans begin to homeschool.

The Heppners begin to homeschool.

Jeanne Newstrom's first trial takes place. Her attorney's arguments are based upon her knowledge and experience and the children's performance, attempting to show that her teaching ability is "essentially equivalent." This evidence is not allowed. She is found guilty of violating the Minnesota Compulsory Attendance Law and sentenced to thirty days in jail or a $300 fine.
(See Appendix A, VII.)
(*Newstrom*)

Newstrom's appeal to the Itasca District Court Panel on the basis of parental rights is also struck down.
(See Appendix A, VII.)
(*Newstrom*)

John Whitehead and Wendell R. Bird write *Home Education and Constitutional Liberties* and a pamphlet called "Home Education: Legislative Solutions to Rights in Conflict," a resource used by Roger Schurke.

July - Kathryn Duerst organizes a conference for Dr. Raymond and Dorothy Moore in Bemidji. She invites Miriam and DuWayne Heppner. The Heppners meet and discuss homeschooling with the Moores in the Duerst's home.
(*Duerst, Heppner*)

The Duersts open the Riverside Schoolhouse Resource Center in Bemidji.

1985

MÂCHÉ's first conference is held at Faith Academy, Fridley, with 300 people in attendance.
(*Schurke, Newhouse*)

The Colemans move to Delaware.

John and Lynne Cooke join the MÂCHÉ board of directors.

The Heppners begin distributing Home Grown Kids resources.

July 19, 1985 - ***State of Minnesota v. Jeanne Newstrom***
The Minnesota Supreme Court reverses the lower courts' rulings. Arguments in this case are made on the basis of the Compulsory Attendance Law being interpreted so inconsistently in the courts of Minnesota. The Supreme Court rules the law is "unconstitutionally vague" in the area of teacher qualifications, and the current law is thrown out, necessitating a new law be written. The court directs the legislature to examine the question and form a new law.
(See Appendix A, VII.)
(*Schurke, Newstrom*)

November 15, 1985 - "Senators Gen Olson, Jude, Waldorf, and Anderson introduce Senate File number 1696, a bill for an act relating to education; revising Minnesota Statutes." This bill is the first attempt to make a new law. It is referred to the Committee on Education.
(See Appendix A, VIII.)
(*Olson, Lindstrom*)

December 12, 1985 - Roger Schurke gives "The Proof is in the Pudding Rather than the Recipe" testimony to the House Education Committee, showing that the results of homeschooling speak for themselves.
(*Roger Schurke's personal notes for the testimony*)

1986

April - MÂCHÉ's 1st Annual Curriculum Fair is held at Crystal Evangelical Free Church, New Hope.

The Duersts take the Home Grown Kids materials to MÂCHÉ's vendor hall for the first time, thus supplying homeschool families with eclectic choices for their curriculum.

MÂCHÉ holds its first graduation ceremony.
(*Cooke, von Gohren*)

June 26, 1986 - Due to the Supreme Court decision on the Newstrom case, a **task force on Compulsory School Attendance** is formed to rewrite Minnesota's law and meets through January 1987 in the Capitol Square Building in St. Paul. Commissioner Ruth E. Randall is elected by unanimous vote as chairperson.
(See Appendix A, IX. a.)
(*Schurke, Olson, Newhouse*)

The Watkinses begin home educating.

The Wetjens begin home educating.

1987

January 12, 1987 - After fourteen meetings over seven months, the **Compulsory School Attendance Task Force** submits its outline for a compulsory education law to the Education Committees for consideration.

(See Appendix A, X.)
(*Olson*)

February 23, 1987 - Representatives McEachern, K. Nelson, Losen, Kostohryz, and Kelso author a **bill in the House on Compulsory Attendance** based on the recommendations of the task force (H.F. 432).
(See Appendix A, XI.)

February 25, 1987 - The House Education Committee meets and discusses the **modification of the Compulsory Attendance Law.** A historical overview is presented by Marsha Gronseth, legal counsel. Recommendations from the **Compulsory School Attendance Task Force** and public testimonies are given.
(See Appendix A, XII.)
(*Olson*)

The House passes the newly proposed Compulsory Attendance Law H.F. 432 and sends it to the Senate for their vote.
(See Appendix A, XIII.)

April 15, 1987 - "The **Senate Education Committee passes H.F. 432**, the House-passed version of the Compulsory Attendance Task Force's recommendations, after testimony by Dr. Lew Finch, Brother William Rhody, and **Roger Schurke**, and many questions and proposed amendments. The bill is sent to the floor by a 16-3 vote."
(See Appendix A, XIII.)
(*Newhouse, Lindstrom, von Gohren, Tuma*)

April - MÂCHÉ's 2nd Annual Curriculum Fair is held at Crystal Evangelical Free Church, New Hope.

April 30, 1987 - The Minnesota Legislature votes on the newly proposed **Compulsory Attendance Law H.F. 432**, and **it passes**. The law is to take effect July 1, 1988. **Homeschooling is legal!** (See Appendix A, XIV.)
(*Newhouse, Lindstrom, von Gohren, Tuma*)

Jerry and Linda McMillin begin homeschooling.

1988

April - MÂCHÉ's 3rd Annual Curriculum Fair is held at Crystal Evangelical Free Church, New Hope.

1989

April - MÂCHÉ's 4th Annual Convention and Curriculum Fair is held at Crystal Evangelical Free Church, New Hope.
Keynote speaker: Michael Farris

MÂCHÉ holds fall meetings in Duluth, Detroit Lakes, and Mankato during October and November.

1990

April - MÂCHÉ's 5th Annual Convention and Curriculum Fair is held at Crystal Evangelical Free Church, New Hope.
Keynote speaker: Robert W. Sweet Jr.

September - MÂCHÉ holds a fall meeting in the metro area at Grace Evangelical Free Church, Fridley.
Featured workshop speakers: Kathryn and David Winters

1991

April - MÂCHÉ's 6th Annual Convention and Curriculum Fair is held at the Crystal Evangelical Free Church, New Hope.
Keynote speaker: Dr. Larry Guthrie

The Watkinses attend their first MÂCHÉ convention.

October and November - MÂCHÉ holds out-state meetings in Bemidji, Crookston, and Austin.

1992

The Heppners buy the Duerst's Home Grown Kids materials and start to officially distribute homeschooling resources.

April - MÂCHÉ's 7th Annual Convention and Curriculum Fair is held at Bloomington Assembly of God.
Keynote speaker: David Quine

Heppner and Heppner Construction exhibits in the MÂCHÉ convention vendor hall for the first time.

Jerry and Pam von Gohren join the MÂCHÉ board of directors

Pam von Gohren becomes MÂCHÉ's legislative liaison

October - MÂCHÉ holds a fall seminar at The Way of the Cross Church, Blaine.

1993

April - MÂCHÉ's 8th Annual Convention and Curriculum Fair is held at Bloomington Assembly of God.
Keynote speaker: Jeff Myers

The Watkinses start helping with MÂCHÉ conventions.

1994

April - MÂCHÉ's 9th Annual Convention and Curriculum Fair is held at Bloomington Assembly of God.
Keynote speakers: The McKim family with their thirteen children from Windom, Texas

Mac and Karen Bryant join the MÂCHÉ board of directors.

Given Hoffman & Eileen Hoffman

1995

April - MÂCHÉ's 10th Annual Convention and Curriculum Fair is held at Bloomington Assembly of God.
Keynote speaker: Dr. Ron Carlson on "Evolution, Dinosaurs, and the Age of the Earth"

Dean and Ruth Lindstrom join the MÂCHÉ board of directors.

Ruth Lindstrom becomes the editor for the MÂCHÉ newsletter.

Dean Lindstrom becomes the MÂCHÉ treasurer.

1996

April - MÂCHÉ's 11th Annual Conference is held in the St. Paul Civic Center for the first time.
Keynote speaker: Jane Hoffman, "The Backyard Scientist"

1997

April - MÂCHÉ's 12th Annual Conference is held in the St. Paul Civic Center.
Keynote speaker: Inge Cannon

Post-Secondary Enrollment Options (PSEO) become more available to homeschoolers.
(*von Gohren, Tuma*)

1998

April - MÂCHÉ's 13th Annual Conference is held in the St. Paul RiverCentre.
Keynote speakers: Dr. Richard Swenson and Michael and Elizabeth Smith

April - The Erpeldings attend their first MÂCHÉ conference.

Fall - The Erpeldings start homeschooling.

1999

April - MÂCHÉ's 14th Annual Conference is held in the St. Paul RiverCentre.

Keynote speaker: Chris Davis

Public school extracurricular activities become available without charge to homeschoolers.

(*von Gohren, Tuma*)

2000

April - MÂCHÉ's 15th Annual Conference is held in the St. Paul RiverCentre.

Keynote speakers: David and Shirley Quine

2001

March 21, 2001 - A **Senate Education Committee Hearing** is held on **Senate Bill 866** which would change homeschool teaching requirements to include a high school diploma and require test scores to be submitted to the school districts. Hundreds of families fill the Minnesota Legislature building to show their support for homeschooling. The bill is defeated.

(See Appendix A, XV.)

(*von Gohren, Tuma, Olson, Erpelding, Bryant*)

April - MÂCHÉ's 16th Annual Conference is held for the **first time** in the Mayo Civic Center, Rochester.

Keynote speakers: Jessica Hulcy and Mark Hamby

May 8, 2001 - The State of Minnesota rules against teaching creation in public schools.

(See Appendix A, XVI.)

The Erpeldings begin serving on the Dodge County Home-schooling Association Board.

2002

April - MÂCHÉ's 17th Annual Conference is held in the Mayo Civic Center, Rochester.
Keynote speaker: Dr. Jeff Myers

David and Linda Watkins join the MÂCHÉ board of directors.

Truancy is changed from a misdemeanor to a petty misdemeanor. This is accomplished by MÂCHÉ's legislative liaison John Tuma working with Amy Klobuchar. Her goal was to help start a program for chronically truant students; Tuma saw an opportunity to protect homeschooling parents from false charges of truancy. (*Tuma*)

John and Lynne Cooke retire from the MÂCHÉ board of directors.

2003

David and Linda Watkins coordinate their first MÂCHÉ conference. Previously the Cookes and Biedermans coordinated the conferences. (Many wonderful volunteers make the MÂCHÉ conference a success.)

April - MÂCHÉ's 18th Annual Conference is held in the St. Paul RiverCentre.
Keynote speaker: Mark Woodhouse

John and Wendy Tuma join the MÂCHÉ board of directors.

2004

April - MÂCHÉ's 19th Annual Conference is held for the **first time** in the Duluth Entertainment and Convention Center (The DECC).
Keynote speaker: Chris Klicka

April - Governor Tim Pawlenty proclaims Saturday, April 17, 2004, "Home Education Day" in Minnesota.
(*original document*)

Roger and Merryl Schurke retire from the MÂCHÉ board of directors.

2005

April - MÂCHÉ's 20th Annual Conference is held in the Mayo Civic Center, Rochester.
Keynote speaker: Dr. S.M. Davis

2006

April - MÂCHÉ's 21st Annual Conference is held in the St. Paul RiverCentre.
Keynote speaker: Rick Green

Brad and Nancy Bjorkman purchase Heppner and Heppner Construction (homeschool resources).

Michael Donnelly starts working for Home School Legal Defense Association (HSLDA).

2007

April - MÂCHÉ's 22nd Annual Conference is held in the Mayo Civic Center, Rochester.
Keynote speaker: Dr. Jay Wile

Summer - The Bjorkmans open Heppner's Legacy Homeschool Resources for business in their store in Elk River.

2008

April - MÂCHÉ's 23rd Annual Conference is held in the DECC, Duluth.
Keynote speaker: Dr. Jeff Myers

2009

April - MÂCHÉ's 24th Annual Conference is held in the St. Paul RiverCentre.

Keynote speaker: Michael Farris, Esq.

Roger and Merryl Schurke are awarded the Friend of Home Education Award.

2010

April - MÂCHÉ's 25th Annual Conference is held in the Mayo Civic Center, Rochester.

Keynote speakers: Drs. Lew and Melodie Sterrett

Cindy Kravik is awarded the Schurke Friend of Home Education Award for her faithful years of service as a support group liaison, chairperson of the Homeschool Helps Booth at the annual MÂCHÉ conference, and member of the Nonpublic Education Council (this council advises the commissioner of education).

Michael Donnelly and John Tuma work on the **"Mandate Reduction Bill"** with Senator Gen Olson.

2011

January 20, 2011 - The **"Home Schools Mandates and Reporting Requirements Reduction"** bill **authored by Gen Olson** is introduced and read in the Senate.

February 3rd, the bill is introduced and read in the House.

February 24th, the House Education Reform Committee recommends "to pass" and refers the bill on to the Education Finance Committee.

(See Appendix A, XVII.)

(*Tuma, Olson, Donnelly*)

April - MÂCHÉ's 26th Annual Conference is held in the DECC, Duluth.

Keynote speaker: Dr. Larry Guthrie

Irene Salo is awarded the Schurke Friend of Home Education Award for her faithful years of service as a support group liaison in Northern Minnesota and her counsel to many homeschoolers.

July 20, 2011 - The **"Home Schools Mandates and Reporting Requirements Reduction"** is passed in House Bill 26. The law substantially reduces reporting requirements for homeschool families and thus extends homeschool freedoms in Minnesota. (See Appendix A, XVII.)
(*Tuma, Olson, Donnelly*)

David Watkins, chairman of MÂCHÉ's working board of directors, becomes executive director of MÂCHÉ under the newly structured policy board.

2012
April - MÂCHÉ's 27th Annual Conference is held in the St. Paul RiverCentre.
Keynote speaker: Phil Downer
Senator Gen Olson is awarded the Schurke Friend of Home Education Award.

Senator Gen Olson retires from the Minnesota Legislature after thirty years of service.

2013
April - MÂCHÉ's 28th Annual Conference is held in the Mayo Civic Center, Rochester.
Keynote speakers: Dr. Henry Morris III and Dr. John Morris
Michael Donnelly is awarded the Schurke Friend of Home Education Award.

2014
April - MÂCHÉ's 29th Annual Conference is held in the DECC, Duluth.

MÂCHÉ's 30th Anniversary!

Keynote speaker: Gregg Harris

Dean and Ruth Lindstrom are awarded the Schurke Friend of Home Education Award.

Chapter One

The Colemans begin homeschooling while it's not yet recognized by the state as a valid means of education. They are reported as truant, but upon identifying themselves as schooling under their church, they are allowed to continue homeschooling their children. They begin to form a homeschool support group, meet the Schurkes, and together start the Minnesota Association of Christian Home Educators (MÂCHÉ) to help and encourage other pioneer homeschool families.

Interview (February 18, 2013) with:
Jim and **Pam Coleman** (Co-Founders of MÂCHÉ)
Children: *Michelle, JoAnna, David, Rebekah, Jeremy, Jonathan, Jennifer, Laura, Julia, Kimberly*

Jim:

We chose to home educate for a practical reason as well as an academic one. We were concerned about the quality of education, and with so many kids, we couldn't afford the Christian school. We figured we could do at least as well as, if not better than, the other options.

Pam:

Not many people were homeschooling at that time [the late 70's and early 80's], but we had friends who were homeschooling their children. They had come to visit us and brought their books and did their thing, and I thought, *This is neat.*

Jim:

Raymond Moore was also instrumental in helping us solidify a lot of our thoughts at the beginning.

Pam:

In 1980 when we started, Michelle was in third grade, and JoAnna was in first grade. They had been attending Powderhorn

Christian School. John Cooke was the principal. We didn't really know a lot about homeschooling, because there wasn't much out there, but after our friends visited us, we started thinking about our options. We said, "Let's try homeschooling for a year and see what happens." We told the Cookes. They were very supportive, and, not that much later, they also started homeschooling.

Jim:

We had heard of one curriculum supplier that might sell to homeschoolers. Back then the companies were worried they'd get in trouble with the private schools. We talked to an A Beka representative and got books. Even then, I think we had to do it under our church, but we were just glad they sold us the books.

Pam:

Michelle and JoAnna loved homeschooling. They especially liked not having to get up and get on the bus.

Jim:

That was my first thought—we won't have to cry anymore when our kids go on the bus the first day.

<u>Legal Concerns</u>

Jim:

Less than six months later, on January 5, 1981, someone reported us to a social worker for not having our kids in school. We received a certified letter from a bunch of lawyers for the public school that said something like, "You're not in compliance," or "Your children are truant," and "Your kids are absent from school without excuse." It was this two-page letter. "Your kids are illegal. We're going to repossess them."

It was intimidating. We thought, *Do we really want to do this? This doesn't sound like where we wanted to go.*

It was time to pray some more.

I called an attorney friend, and he said, "Put a letter on church stationery. Tell them it's under the church, and that should take care of it." We did and became Great Commission Academy.

I responded January 9 with, "I should like to inform you that my children, Michelle and JoAnna, have been in private school since September of 1980, when they transferred from Powderhorn Christian School. It's my understanding that both Minnesota law and federal law include a clause for the strict separation of church and state. Under the jurisdiction of a congregation of Christians, we are operating in accordance with the laws of the land, etc."

Over a month later we got a much calmer letter back, essentially saying, "Send us the details." We sent them details on our curriculum, our school day, and all that. They said, "We want to send somebody out."

Pam:

The man who came was very nice. It was pretty scary though. I don't think we really thought much about the legal issues until we got into the middle of it. I guess we had heard stories of parents being arrested, but we didn't really think it would ever happen to us. And thankfully, it didn't.

Jim:

They let us do what we were doing, yet in 1982, they were still saying they were confident that superior education opportunities for our kids were available in the public school. I have a little feistiness in me, so I wrote this back to the deputy superintendent.

Dear Mr. Phillips,

If you care to take the time, I would be most interested to hear from you, specifically, why and how superior education opportunities are available for Michelle and JoAnna in the public schools. Perhaps some dialogue on this opinion could benefit a growing number of parents who are increasingly dissatisfied with the quality of public school education.

I personally was raised exclusively in the public school system, including college, but I see many changes which frankly steer me away from this setting, especially for younger children who are more influenced by the character of their teachers and peers than by words in a textbook. At the same time, I recognize the threat to public school education of population decrease in general, and more and more parents sending their youngsters to private schools. As with many others, I am willing to put my dollars and time into what I consider to be the best opportunity for my own children to receive a thorough education in the ABCs, as well as character development.

Thankful to be an American with such a choice available to me,

Jim Coleman

We never heard back from them.

When it comes to raising your own kids, you think more about the bad things that go on in the school system. One of the dumbest objections to home education was socialization. I majored in sociology, and one of the reasons you homeschool is for the socializing of the children properly instead of improperly.

Pam:

One thing that really convinced me about homeschool versus the Christian school was our daughter JoAnna. In first grade, she came home and told me about something her teacher had said. It sounded wrong. I said, "You must have misunderstood her." But JoAnna would not believe me. She was going to go with her teacher rather than her mother, and though the teacher was a wonderful lady, I thought, *This is not how it should be.* With JoAnna only in first grade, I thought, *What is this going to be like in the future?*

Jim:

You only get one chance to raise your kids, and everybody starts out as an amateur. To me, character as a Christian was the number-one thing we wanted to instill in our kids. Character qualities last for a lifetime. Character helps them get employment, helps them in life, and helps them in marriage. Our Christian character also counts in our interactions in our community, because people will see Christ in us. To me that's more important than the ABCs, the three Rs, and all that other stuff.

Starting MÂCHÉ
Jim:

When we started home educating there was a dearth of help or support groups. We figured there had to be others who were either already home educating or were thinking about it and could benefit from a support group. We had met and hit it off with Roger and Merryl Schurke, and together we kicked around the idea of starting something.

They knew a couple of families in Minnesota who were home educating, and we said, "Let's see what happens if we try to have a gathering of some sort."

On November 29, 1983, we had our first meeting for the Minnesota Association of Christian Home Educators at Powderhorn Park (where we were meeting for church).

Pam:

We had like forty or fifty people come.

Jim:

There were way more people interested than we thought. We still have the original letter that went out, announcing that first meeting. It's like the Declaration of Independence.

From that meeting, MÂCHÉ came together, and we were off and running.

The verse in Deuteronomy, "Train up a child," is what we used as our foundation for home educating. That is why "Christian" is in the name of the organization, because we were, and we wanted that. I don't think it ever hurts to raise our flag of Christianity, because the world needs light, and that's no less true now than it was then.

In 1984, we sent out a fledgling MÂCHÉ newsletter. We didn't do color; we used colored paper. It was very archaic. The newsletter was sent out no more than monthly and was meant to encourage and inform. I'd write a little spiritual column. We also had other people write. Roger Schurke always wrote the legal help. He kept up with what the legislature was thinking of doing, and he let us know if there was a fire to put out or something to go rally over.

"...bring them up in the discipline and instruction of the Lord."
- Ephesians 6:4b NASB

Dear Friends:

You are invited to the initial meeting of the Minnesota Association of Christian Home Educators.

Date: Tuesday, November 29, 1983

Time: 7:15 p.m.

Place: Powderhorn Park Building
at the corner of 15th Avenue South
and East 34th Street, Minneapolis

What is it all about?

- Meet other home educators

- Formation of local support groups and prayer chain

- Share ideas, teaching aids and curriculum information

- Announcement of upcoming home education seminar

- Discussion of legal and political status of home education locally, regionally and nationally

- Answers to the questions you may have

We have felt a need to be united in a Christ-centered support group for some months. It is our hope to develop a local network of members who can encourage one another more regularly and practically in reaching Christian goals with their children.

Please help us get the word out. Invite others you know who are interested or who are teaching their children in the home. Please feel free to call us for more information.

Sincerely,

Jim Coleman
Pastor
(612) 722-4604

Roger Schurke
Attorney
(612) 822-1082

Original document. Jim Coleman, "It's like the Declaration of Independence."

Minnesota Association of
Christian Home Educators

The Minnesota Association of Christian Home Educators (MACHE) was formed in 1983 to encourage Christian families in the education of their children according to Biblical principles. It is the desire of MACHE members to learn and to practice the ways of the Lord, as recorded in God's Word, the Bible. It is our intention to pass on to our children a godly heritage, and to "bring them up in the discipline and instruction of the Lord." (Eph 6:4b NASB)

MACHE is, therefore, supportive of parents who have chosen to educate their children at home. As a statewide association, it is our goal to be spiritually refreshing as well as to aid the process of education. Input from members is continually desired in order to more fully impact quality education in Minnesota.

MACHE members enjoy these benefits:

* newsletters published periodically to further inform you in academic, Biblical, and legal matters relating to home education.

* quarterly meetings for encouragement and greater opportunity to "grow" as a home educator. (Also, possible contact with other MACHE members or other home schoolers in your local area.)

* workshops and seminars designed to further equip parents in successful home education.

* special educational field trips to involve your children with other "home grown kids".

* annual picnic to meet many other home educating families and enjoy the many talents represented by our children.

* certificate of membership.

To join, send your name, address, and $7.00 (annual fee) to:
MACHE, Box 14326, Mpls., MN. 55414

Original Document. MÂCHÉ Membership and Benefits

At the very beginning, MÂCHÉ membership was seven dollars. The fee for the first MÂCHÉ conference for members was two dollars. Six dollars for nonmembers, but if they registered and paid their fee, it was nine dollars.

We had our first workshop April 7, 1984, at Grace Church of Edina. We were shocked. A lot of people [360 plus] came to it—not at the civic center like it is now (we've never even been to that giant thing)—but it's amazing how from small beginnings sometimes things just catch fire.

It was the right time. There were lots of people thinking about and seeing homeschooling in a positive way. MÂCHÉ took off, and we give God the credit.

Pam:

The MÂCHÉ homeschool picnic is a favorite memory. It was a fun day, tubing down the Apple River.

Jim:

Doing things together was great, not only for the added socialization of the kids, but because we were with other people who thought like we did.

You have to remember, this was a pioneer movement. People didn't have the camaraderie and resources they do now. Just finding another homeschooling family was exciting, and the early meetings were exhilarating, if not for the quality of speakers and size, just for that camaraderie. Without that camaraderie, you were just kind of out there on your own, hoping you didn't get in trouble.

Pam:

We used to get a lot of phone calls.

Jim:

People didn't have too many places to go to get their questions answered. When you get into home educating, you don't know for sure how you are going to do it, and there is an awful lot of on-the-job training. Those little crumb grabbers that we adore and challenge, challenge us. You find out this works, this doesn't, and the support group stuff like MÂCHÉ is extremely helpful.

The greatest benefit I've felt was just the interaction of like-minded folks who are also struggling, and now you're struggling in a team setting instead of all by yourself. That was huge for us. To have people in our state and in our city who were also seeking to teach their kids God's way. We weren't involved with MÂCHÉ for very long though.

Pam:

In 1985, two years after starting MÂCHÉ, we moved to Delaware.

Jim:

We looked for a state home education organization out there, but there was none. So we started a homeschooling organization out there too. Whether it's still alive or not, I don't know.

Pam:

I think we got more phone calls when we lived there than when we lived in Minnesota. Today, it's great to see homeschooling being so much more accepted and well-known.

Jim:

It's very proven now. They can't challenge the academics or the character.

Pam:

It is proven to be successful, but we can't take our freedom for granted. It's important to realize that homeschooling is not something that we can assume we will always have, because there is opposition. People will be against it.

Jim:

A verse that encouraged us early on is "I can do all things through Christ who strengthens me." That's not changed, and so whatever future obstacles come in front of people who want to school their kids, God will have an answer. He is faithful, and trusting Him and clinging to Him is the only way to get through the process.

There are days that everything goes wrong and the kids are gnarly and the books don't come on time. There are days where you just think, *Why are we doing this? I could just put them on that yellow bus and watch Oprah*, but the parents gain more than the kids. That is always true whether you're teaching a Sunday school class or anything else. The teacher learns more than the pupil.

Maybe the greatest benefit to home education is the benefit that the parents get. There is such a great delight to parents in the end result and seeing, "My kids turned out. We did something right! They didn't have to have a public high school stamp. They can actually get jobs. They can actually go to college. They can even get scholarships. They can even get the first full-ride scholarship ever at a college!" One of our daughters did. These kinds of achievements make you happy as a parent.

Pam:

Another benefit of homeschooling was the closeness of the family. Our kids are good friends with each other. Not that they don't ever have any problems, but our family has really remained close.

Jim:

Our kids got that family bonding, and now they want that in their families. They want that closeness and that continuity. The blessings just keep coming. We're done but not finished. We're still reaping all of that sowing, in the lives of our kids and the lives of our grandkids.

<u>Advice</u>

Jim:

To use a stolen analogy, you don't push the baby bird out of the nest and hope they can figure out how to fly before they crash. You wait until you're sure they know what to do to fly. If nature is smart enough to do that, maybe we should be.

Pam:

If I had it to do over with homeschooling, I wouldn't be so structured in the books and do every little page and workbook. I'd do more hands-on things.

Jim:

Proverbs 3:5-6 says, "Trust in the Lord with all of your heart, do not lean on your own understanding; in all your ways acknowledge Him, and He will make your path straight." That sure bodes well for schooling at home and everything else in life. God wants to walk alongside of us through this life, and guide us, and guard us, and equip us for what is over the next hill.

Pam:

Don't give up. Never, never, never give up—even though your day seems like it's not going to turn out.

Jim:

God's strength is sufficient. My favorite verse is "My grace is sufficient for you." That's present tense—that's why I like it. "My grace is sufficient for you." There is nothing you can't do when you have His grace.

Chapter Two

The Schurkes begin homeschooling during a time when the legality of homeschooling under the Minnesota Compulsory Attendance Law is being left to interpretation. After working with Mike Farris in Washington, the Shurkes move back to Minnesota and connect with the Colemans. Together they start MÂCHÉ. Two years later, Roger joins the attorney representing one of two families who are fighting for the right to homeschool before the Minnesota Supreme Court. The court rules the Compulsory Attendance Law unconstitutionally vague, and a Compulsory School Attendance Task Force, of which Roger Schurke is a member, is formed to help create what becomes the new Compulsory Attendance Law in 1987.

Interview (January 23, 2013) with:
Roger and **Merryl Schurke** (Co-Founders of MÂCHÉ)
Children: *Kristin, Christopher, Christian, Nathanael*

Merryl:

We came back to Minnesota for a visit from Texas in 1977, when we saw a headline in the Minneapolis paper that there was a family, the Hattenpaas, in Schroeder, Minnesota, who were teaching their kids at home and being taken to court for it. We were heading that direction, so we stopped in and visited with them. We were so impressed.

The wife had a tenth-grade education and her husband had only completed eighth grade. Their children were amazing. They could talk about anything and knew so much about so many different things. We were really impressed with the education these children had been receiving.

Two or three years later, we were living in International Falls, and the day before our daughter was to start fourth grade, Roger said, "Why don't we just teach her at home?" I said, "Are you crazy? There's no way we can start teaching her at home. I don't have any books. I wouldn't know where to begin." He said, "We don't have to start tomorrow." You can't argue with a lawyer. Roger said, "We can ask my mom to see if she can get some books from a school in Minneapolis and send them to us to get started." I said, "Okay."

Roger:

We had been in a ministry called The Agape Force in Lindale, Texas, and they had an elementary school. Our daughter did really well there, but then I took a job as a city attorney in International Falls. She ended up in a public school, and we saw things developing in her we didn't like, peer group related things. That was part of my impetus in thinking perhaps we could do better if we homeschooled her.

I couldn't see a real reason not to. I knew we could do it, based on what I had learned from seeing the Hattenpaas and others. The other tie-in is my mom had connections to John Cooke, who was the principal of Powderhorn Christian School. That's where my mom got the books we initially used.

Legal Issues
Roger:

A lot of people questioned the legality of what we were doing, but I had no problem with that. My response to authorities was "If you want to do something, take me to court." They never did. I loved it.

In International Falls, the superintendent called and asked what we were doing. I told him, "I believe it's totally legal. We have several U.S. Supreme Court cases backing what we are doing. Even though there is not a specific law in Minnesota that says we can, there is not one that says we can't. So this is what we are going to do. You know who I am. So let it be. I won't cave or roll over for you." He never bothered us again.

13

Merryl:

The principal called though and said, "I'm calling because I need to know if your daughter is enrolled in school." I said, "Yes, she is," because I had a book with our school name, Cedar Creek Christian School, and her name was written in it. So she was enrolled in school. He said, "Thank you. That's all I want to know." And he hung up immediately.

Roger:

They didn't want to deal with us.

Merryl:

I remember that first year having to re-adjust my whole lifestyle in order to teach our kids at home. It meant sacrificing some things I enjoyed at the time. But I have plenty of time now to do those things, and I loved being able to spend those years with our kids.

Roger:

In 1981, we moved to Rushford, Minnesota. The superintendent there was threatening to take another homeschooling family to court.

Merryl:

They had heard about us and decided to teach their kids at home too, and the superintendent tried to get them in trouble. With Roger's law degree and my elementary education degree, the superintendent didn't want to bother with us, but anybody else better watch out.

Roger:

I called him and said, "Now why don't you take me to court? I think that would be more fair." On Easter Sunday that year, the Winona paper had a write-up on home education. My photo and the superintendent's photo were in the family section of the Winona paper. We were each telling our side of the story. It went into depth about what my position was and what his was. He never did take anyone to court.

After leaving Rushford, we moved to Washington State [1982], and I worked with Mike Farris in Olympia for a year. Mike was working with Tim and Beverly LaHaye [who were associated with what was known as the Moral Majority].

I also spent time with Raymond and Dorothy Moore while we were there. Raymond Moore was a very dynamic individual. Gregg Harris was actually working for them when I met him. And we miss Chris Klicka, that's for sure. Sweet guy.

Merryl:

When we moved to Washington, we had three kids, all five years apart. In public school they would have been on different buses and at different schools. I don't think they would have even known each other. We had our fourth child while we were there, and Kristin, our oldest, was, I think, in seventh grade.

Mike Farris came over one day, and he said, "Have you ever had your daughter tested to see how she's doing?" We had been teaching her for three or four years by then. I said, "I haven't had any opportunity or reason to." Mike said, "Well, how do you know she's learning?" I said, "I'm with her every day. I'm doing the tests from the books, and I can tell she's learning."

He said, "Wouldn't you like to know how she compares with other children in the United States?" I said, "Well, if you have a test, I'll give it to her." I'd done it before as a teacher. He said, "I'll get you a standardized achievement test, and you can give it to her." So I did. She scored post-high school on everything, which was shocking to me. I had no clue she had learned that much at home. Mike was also quite impressed.

Working with Mike Farris

Roger:

One day Mike told me he had a vision in the shower to start this homeschool defense organization. That's how HSLDA [Home School Legal Defense Association] got started, Mike's shower vision. Mike is a multifaceted individual who can multitask like you wouldn't believe. He's always looking for more and more to do; that's the way he operates. We went through the process of Mike deciding to move the HSLDA office. We debated Texas, possibly Minnesota. They ended up in Virginia.

Starting MÂCHÉ

Roger:

At that point in time, we moved back to Minnesota and started looking for a homeschool organization. Jim and Pam Coleman had a group of people interested in homeschooling who were meeting at their home. I attended, and it was the strangest group of people. The Colemans were Christians, and I think one other couple was, but the rest of the people were not. I left that meeting really chagrined.

I called Jim Coleman and said, "Jim, I appreciate your desire to start a homeschool organization, but it can't be with these people. What do you say we start a Christian one?" Jim jumped on it, and that's how MÂCHÉ started. We used Jim's basement for an office. We had a cigar box for our records and for whatever cash we had.

Our first meeting was in 1983 at Powderhorn Park in Minneapolis. Probably about a hundred people showed up.

Merryl:

I think it was a list of about forty, and with spouses it probably was close to a hundred.

Roger:

The first MÂCHÉ conference was at Faith Academy in Fridley in 1985. I remember I asked the crowd, "How many of you are teachers here?" About half the audience raised their hands, which indicated to me they were unhappy with what they saw in the school systems.

Merryl:

For the first conferences we would bring boxes of donuts and coffee ourselves. We didn't have caterers or vendors or anything. It was all of us working together and putting it all together.

We would also have parties every month for the newsletter, this little trifold thing. We'd have the Biedermans and some other families come over with their kids, and we would address the newsletters by hand and get them all set to mail out.

Newsletter of the Minnesota Association of
Vol. / No. / Christian Home Educators

Reflections on Our First Year
by Lori Voeller

Do you feel you are called by God to home educate your children? Home education should not be something one drifts into or decides to do in order to get out of something else. It should be as surely a call from God as is a call to the mission field, or to full-time Christian service. When I realized deep within my heart that our homeschool is a call from God, my attitudes changed. When things become difficult, I can believe it is part of God's plan to perfect us, to help us know Him, to strengthen us to work through the difficulties, and to be fruitful for Him.

Many parents have started their home school with much fear of being discovered by the authorities. This has not been a concern of ours, nor will it be any time, because we are called of God to be home educators. He is the umbrella for our school and He has given us a spirit of boldness - not timidity. Fear is something terribly contagious and easily caught by our children. Our first lesson to our children was to teach them to have a sense of healthy pride towards being educated at home. We rejoice to see how continuously thankful our seven year old is to us and the Lord for his home education.

The First MÂCHÉ Newsletter

Roger:

We own some property on the Apple River by Somerset, Wisconsin, and we used to have MÂCHÉ picnics there. We don't have those anymore, obviously, but they were really a good time. Families would come out, and we would float down the river, play volleyball or horseshoes, have kids' relay races, and what have you. Sometimes we'd spend the night there. Those were good times.

MÂCHÉ's growth was phenomenal. I anticipated home-schooling would grow, because of my association with HSLDA and seeing how that was growing. I wasn't at all surprised when it did. I did find it overwhelming at times, because we would get, no joke, forty phone calls a day from people with questions. I was trying to work as a lawyer out of our home and also answer all these calls. It was crazy. There were always two questions that were asked: "Is it legal?" and "What about socialization?" I became very adept at answering both.

Every year the number of people attending MÂCHÉ conferences increased. One year it was held on a cold, snowy day at Edina West High School. For several years we had it at Crystal Free Church, but we quickly graduated to larger facilities. Innumerable hours were put in by many people to make the conferences a success.

The initial MÂCHÉ board was us, Jim and Pam Coleman, and Jim and Laurie Voeller. The Voellers went to the Philippines, and the Colemans moved to Delaware. The Smiths joined the board, and I think it was in the late eighties the Cookes were asked to join, as well. The Lindstroms joined us in the nineties.

We had, I think, for a number of years, the oldest homeschool board in the world. I might have almost been the youngest person on the board for a while, only because I'm six months younger than Merryl.

Merryl:

[*Laughs*] Five.

Roger:

Excuse me, five months.

When Mac and Karen Bryant joined the board they were a little younger than the rest of us. The Watkinses joined after that, and I was so happy when I was able to tell Dave Watkins he could take over my role.

We had served on the board for over twenty years. You know, once you get into it so far, you don't really get out. When we first started MÂCHÉ, we didn't have a director. It was just Jim and me. Eventually I became the director, then John Cooke was for a time, and then that responsibility came back to me until 2004, when David Watkins became chairman of the board.

Newstrom and Budke Cases
Roger:

In 1982, John Eidsmoe was contacted by the Budkes, a Catholic homeschool family who had gone to county court without an attorney and lost. They appealed in 1983 and went to the Minnesota State Supreme Court in 1985, along with the Newstrom family, who weren't religious. Combined, these two families made a very interesting case.

During that case, I went with John Eidsmoe when he did his oral argument before the Minnesota Supreme Court. The Supreme Court ruled that the existing Compulsory Attendance Law was so vague it was unconstitutional. The basis of their opinion was not Frist Amendment rights, but the vagueness of the law and that we were being denied equal protection under the law because of the vagueness of the law.

They told the legislature, "You have to make a new law that people understand." So the then-commissioner of education, Ruth Randall, made a task force to write a new law (1986).

The Compulsory School Attendance Task Force
Roger:

There were twelve people on the task force. I was one, along with Bethany Newhouse, and another was the Anoka County district superintendent, Lew Finch. We were at odds, he and

I, partially because I lived in his school district and partially because we're both type A people.

On the task force, he represented the public school side pretty strongly, but he had a softer side too that most didn't recognize.

We had a lot of pro-homeschool people who would just attend the task force deliberations. Several people were there a lot and had a lot of input. Retired Senator Gen Olson is a huge contributor to homeschooling. Gen was the driving force to push that bill through the Senate. We just gave her an award last spring. She is a sweetheart.

Pam von Gohren was also there. She's a hard worker. We needed her. She and her husband, Jerry, were members of the MÂCHÉ board.

On the task force, we also had Brother Rhody, who was with the Catholic schools. He strongly helped us because he had such a heavy interest in the private school side. What I tried to do in all my task force deliberations was identify homeschools as private schools. That was my whole thrust. I didn't want to separate us out on a branch all by ourselves so they could lop us off. I wanted to drag us into the private school sector as much as possible.

The different debate issues went back and forth. We'd say, "We'll allow standardized achievement testing." Then they'd say, "Who's going to give the test?" "Let's be realistic. Who do you want to give the tests? The commissioner of education?"

I remember they wanted a specific standardized achievement test. I said, "No, we'll go with any accredited standardized achievement test," of which there are probably fifty. So I knew we were okay there. I also knew the next issue would be "What about the results? Are we entitled to them?" There was nothing in the law that said parents had to turn the results over to the school district.

They kept saying, "Well, how will we really know they've given the tests?" I said, "You're just going to have to accept at face value that the parents have administered the test."

The testing is really for the parents. It's for them for a number of different reasons. One of which is, in case they are taken to court, they can prove their kids have been learning. Another one is if your child is having problems, you know about it.

The Law of 1987
Roger:

I had a lot to do with drafting the law's specific language. I created it by looking at and incorporating laws from other states that were similar, and of course John Eidsmoe helped. Mike Smith might have helped me with it some. I don't remember.

In any event, it worked. The task force made the recommendation, and the 1987 Minnesota Legislature passed it into law. As a result of that law, I think people felt a lot freer to homeschool.

Memorable Moments Homeschooling
Roger:

My youngest brother would always analyze things, and homeschooling kind of ran against the grain with him. He came to me one day, and he said, "I want to talk to you." I thought, *Here we go.*

He said, "I've been watching your children as they have been homeschooled, and I have got to tell you, I'm really surprised. I thought they would be misfits and be poorly educated. But really, they are just doing great. I love their personalities. I love the way they interact with people, and it's obvious to me they are very intelligent and learning. So, all I can do is congratulate you on making that choice." I'm going, *Wow, didn't expect that.* So that's a real memory, to say the least.

We took vacations at times of the year when most people couldn't. We'd be at these campgrounds, and older people would ask, "What are you doing here? Are you on the run from the law?" In the eighties, I had some pretty long hair and a full beard. I looked like I could've been. But then these older people would meet our kids, and they'd tell us, "I can't wait to get home and tell my kids about this homeschool thing." It was like advertising homeschooling.

Merryl:

When our oldest son was thirteen, he did the wiring in the house which we remodeled. So we got to the electricity section in science, and he said, "I already know all of this, Mom." I said, "You're right. You do!"

Roger:

I guess the sum total, the highlight of homeschooling, was seeing the product of it. My saying, which I've carried with me to many MÂCHÉ conferences, is "The proof is in the pudding, not the recipe." Don't tell me you have to teach them a certain way. I want to see what the result is.

Advice

Roger:

I would encourage large families. It's my understanding that the size of the family is decreasing, and that's fewer kids to impact the world.

Merryl:

Use technology in a positive way, and yet be careful not to let it overtake your lives.

Roger:

Before you start homeschooling, be sure you know what you are getting into. Be sure you are willing to pay the price, because it's not easy.

Merryl:

I would say, keep your heart and mind focused on the Lord. Let Him lead you, and He will guide you and direct your path and show you the way. And He will bring you success.

Chapter Three

Michael Farris begins homeschooling and meets Roger Schurke. He founds the Home School Legal Defense Association (HSLDA) and begins helping homeschoolers around the country with legal issues involving homeschooling.

Interview (September 26, 2013) with:
Michael Farris (HSLDA Chairman)

Mike:

I was in Olympia, Washington, running an organization called the Bill of Rights Legal Foundation. It had previously been known as the Moral Majority of Washington State, and Roger Schurke helped me as a volunteer part-time.

Roger was an attorney and a pharmacist, and he was homeschooling. He was the second homeschool parent I ever met. The first was when I looked in the mirror. My wife and I had just started homeschooling, and we learned that Roger and Merryl were homeschooling. Their kids were a little older. It was a real encouragement to meet another family that was homeschooling, and they had been at it for a year or two. So they were the veterans. We had been at it for several weeks.

I remember distinctly, we were over at their house for dinner, and I said to Roger, "Where are we going to get high school diplomas?" He said, "Well, where do you think the public schools get them? At a print shop." And I thought, *Cool.*

One reason HSLDA sells high school diplomas is because of Roger's advice. I knew we could go to a print shop and get them. Every time I think of high school diplomas, I think of Roger.

Roger and I would often talk about stuff while playing golf. He is an incredibly good golfer. He and Mike Smith are both incredibly good golfers, but Roger probably is a little bit better. Roger was a real encouragement to me, just to have another person who had been at homeschooling a little bit longer and had older kids. They had an eleven-year-old they were homeschooling. It was pretty amazing. They had good kids. They were sharp kids. Even though I tease about their cookie-cutter type names, they were not cookie-cutter kids. These were very individualistic kids. They had a really healthy family. I liked what I saw, and that helped solidify where I was going.

HSLDA

Mike:

The concept of HSLDA's original logo was Roger's. He got a graphic artist friend to design it for us. The logo was a mom and dad, little boy, and little girl, all silhouettes. The little boy had his baseball cap turned sideways, and the little girl had a doll. About five years later, we determined we should add more kids to the logo since many homeschool families have more than two children.

Although Mike Smith and I, along with our wives, were the original four board members for HSLDA, Roger was there at the beginning, giving advice, and I think he proofread our original Articles of Incorporation. We hoped HSLDA would grow really fast so that we would have enough funds to pay Roger to be an attorney for HSLDA, but that didn't happen. However, by the time MÂCHÉ started, HSLDA had become strong enough to help state organizations by providing encouragement and legal support.

MÂCHÉ

Mike:

I have always felt MÂCHÉ was an especially strong organization. They had Roger, but they had other people, too, who were really very significant in the homeschool community. HSLDA's role was as advisor and backstop to help MÂCHÉ.

To me, MÂCHÉ is one of the best-run state organizations, especially in their ability to understand and manage the nuances of politics. I don't think we ever had to litigate a case in Minnesota. I know we had to help stomp out fires once in a while, but the good teamwork between MÂCHÉ and HSLDA made that relatively easy.

<u>Advice</u>

Mike:

"Always bring your friends with." Good advice even though in most other parts of the country nobody else says "with" at the end of the sentence. That is a Minnesota thing.

Build relationships, because those relationships matter. You never know what could happen. I recently spoke with an Iowa senator who took my high school constitutional law course. Now here he is as an adult, helping my Convention of States project. Little seeds we plant; they'll grow. Last week the guy who was a lobbyist for the ACLU called me and wanted to talk about how to fix the UN Convention on the Rights of Persons with Disabilities. This connection was the result of seeds sown in 1992, 1994. That's a long time ago, politically speaking, but I've learned, treat those who disagree with you with kindness. Yes, you must stand your ground and agree with them when you can, but be professional and principled.

When you plant seeds, you never have any idea how long it's going to be before they pay dividends. Thanks to the support of homeschoolers, I was able to work really hard to pass the Religious Freedom Restoration Act in Congress. Bill Clinton signed it into law in 1993. Recently, that law was used successfully to defend Hobby Lobby in their desire to avoid paying for abortions in their medical coverage. The Religious Freedom Restoration Act gave them protection even though the Supreme Court's views on religious freedom had failed.

I would encourage people to be willing to plant little seeds and take action. Realize that we are in a long-term battle. You will see fruit way down the road. The job we face is bigger and brighter, and yet more difficult and more frustrating; it's more of everything, the good and the bad. Realize that small seeds grow to be big plants. Have a long-term view of things. Be faithful and be patient.

Chapter Four

The Biedermans start homeschooling before it is considered legal, join the MÂCHÉ board of directors, and help out with MÂCHÉ newsletters and conferences.

Written Contribution Submitted (December 13, 2013) by:
Carl and **Carla Biederman** (Past MÂCHÉ Board Members)
Children: *Sara, Christi, Karen, Deanna, Nathan, Mark*

Carla:

I still remember the excitement of our youngest daughter running to the door saying, "Mommy, the EP Mess man is here with our books!"

In 1984, our homeschooling journey began, as did a friendship with Roger and Merryl Schurke. We asked if they'd be willing to meet and answer all of our many questions. It didn't take long for us to develop a friendship, and before long Roger asked us to join them and several other couples for a board meeting of the official Minnesota Association of Christian Home Educators!

Joining the MÂCHÉ Board of Directors

Carla:

Our initial board of directors began with several couples, eventually settling in with three families—Schurkes, Cookes, and us.

Our best memories of those early years were our three families working together on the state conferences, which were held in local churches—until we outgrew them. We cherished the friendships from all over the country. We worked together as a family, from hand painting the signs for the "Curriculum Fair" to answering phone calls, licking stamps, and addressing one-page conference brochures.

Should it surprise us now that our children are not afraid of tackling just about anything? Philippians 4:13 has been a favorite verse: "I can do all things through Christ Jesus who gives me strength!"

Chapter Five

The Duersts attend a seminar presented by the Moores, the grandparents of the modern homeschooling movement. The Duersts then host the Moores for a seminar in Bemidji, after which the Duersts start a small book business selling the Moores' books. They start vending at homeschool conferences as the Home Grown Kids booth, and the business grows as they add other helpful books to their inventory. Eventually they buy an old schoolhouse for a store-front and become the Riverside Schoolhouse Resource Center. They retire from the business by selling the best of their stock to the Heppner family, who start vending for themselves at homeschool conferences as Heppner and Heppner Construction.

Interview (November 26, 2013) with:

Kathryn Duerst (Riverside Schoolhouse Resource Center—*a.k.a.* Home Grown Kids)

   Husband: *Dan*

   Children: *Bethany, Sarah, Anna, Rebecca, Timothy, Andrew, Philip*

Kathy:

It was the year 1983 that I heard Dr. Moore on the radio while I was down in the Twin Cities. It was an interview in which he was announcing an upcoming event, in which Dr. Moore and his wife were going to be presenting this idea of homeschooling.

The event was going to take place in the Black Hills, close to the date of my birthday. I thought, *That could be my birthday present.* I said to my husband, "Dan, this is so exciting! It's around my birthday, and I've always wanted to see the Black Hills, the mountains, and everything! We could take a family trip and also get in on this seminar!"

We actually went. It was a fairly small group. Afterward, each of the families in attendance went back to their respective cities and was contacted the following year by Dr. Moore. He asked if we would like to be coordinators for an event, each in our own city.

The Moores in Bemidji

Kathy:

I looked into it, did the research, and said, "You know we could pull in a crowd all the way from Canada, Fargo, and the Cities. We can set it up at the Beaux Arts Ballroom at Bemidji State University and get it on the radio." I got the word out every which way I could, and so of course, everyone I could think of was invited.

We had it on July 15, 1984. About three hundred and fifty people attended, and the Moores had me go up and introduce them on the stage.

Afterward, I was asked to write an article for one of the very beginning MÂCHÉ newsletters, summarizing the seminar, which I did. Dr. Moore and Dorothy were pleased with it, saying it represented their presentation very well.

The best part, though, about doing the seminar was that the Moores stayed in our home. I loved the time they spent with us and the way Dorothy Moore would share about their principles. She talked about reading to children from infancy.

They both shared about the way children internalize and establish their values, and how that comes from a balance of work and learning.

They talked about teachable moments, when your children ask a question and you go find out the answer together. You sit down for a few minutes, as long as their attention span holds, and you give them the information at that teachable moment.

One thing Dr. Moore was big on was a routine where the children can get used to something, and they can predict it. Routine is a form of security in which children thrive, and within that routine there are certain values being lived out consistently.

If children haven't established and internalized their value systems, they tend to get confused. They don't become leaders; they become followers. If you want them to be a light in the world, then you need to train them in the way that they should go, and then they will not depart from it.

Originally, I was sure my children were going to go to Christian school. I was even involved in the debates they were having over a local Christian school and later served on the school board. On one side was the thought, "We can't abandon the public schools. We have to be a light, and our children have to be a light."

I said, "Well, the teachers could maybe be strong enough to be the light in the public schools, and some of the older children who are strongly established in their faith and values maybe could." But when you've got a young child and—this is what I got from Dr. Moore, about the greenhouse—if that young child is in their formative development, you don't put that young plant out in the storm. You keep them in the greenhouse until they are mature enough to handle the storm.

Those are some of the things I learned from spending that special time with Raymond and Dorothy Moore.

Dr. Raymond and Dorothy Moore also had a little line of Home Grown Kids materials, and they asked us if we wanted to be distributors. We signed up before they even left town and started with that small line of just the materials they recommended.

The very first display we had we set up in the corner of our living room in our house in town. Neighbors, friends, and people we had met through the homeschooling movement or at the seminar would come by and look at our books. We were all new to this, and we were learning together.

Home Grown Kids Booth at MÂCHÉ
Kathy:

In those early years, we started finding the different organizations that would welcome our display. I contacted MÂCHÉ, and we brought our display there. It started out small, as the Home Grown Kids booth with the Moore's materials, but each year, as we became familiar with other materials, it grew bigger. Eventually, it was six tables long and quite an extravagant and beautiful display. We met many wonderful people and learned so much!

We started with the homeschool conventions and later branched out to Sunday school conventions, and eventually we started going into other states. We went to Gregg Harris's presentations as far as the West Coast, and we went down all the way to Texas.

The spring of 1990 was our last display at MÂCHÉ, and the summer of 1990 was our last display in Texas.

Selling to the Heppners

Kathy:

What we offered got very extensive, but the cream of the crop is what Heppners wanted. They didn't want the one-of-everything display. So they chose out what they wanted when they bought the business in 1992.

Advice

Kathy:

One thing I commonly say is "You get the heart, you get the whole person." If you don't get the heart of the child, you haven't got any of them. The point of gaining the heart is to present the whole person to Christ (Proverbs 4:23; 2 Corinthians 11:2).

Chapter Six

Jeanne Newstrom puts her kids in public school in the mornings and does home-based education in the afternoons. She is summoned to court and told her kids are required to be in school full-time. She loses in both the county court and the district court and appeals to the Minnesota Supreme Court, where her case is joined with the Budke's case. Their lawyers argue the vagueness of the law, and the court reverses the ruling on Jeanne's case and throws out the law on the basis of its being unconstitutionally vague.

Interview (January 7, 2013) with:
Jeanne Newstrom (An Innovative Educator)
        Husband: *Tim*
        Children: *Katy, Dawn, Flora*

Jeanne:

My husband, Tim, and I are from north Hennepin County. We moved to the Grand Rapids area in 1978, when Katy was four and Dawn was two.

When we lived in the Twin Cities, I was very involved with the La Leche League, which was very influential to me.

The La Leche League is an international organization of mothering through breastfeeding. Our most important function was coaching women that they were the person best suited to make decisions for their family. They knew their baby, themselves, their family situation, and their husband better than anybody else. We encouraged being attentive to your child rather than following someone else's rules about what you should be doing.

When I was in high school, I was fascinated by the research that was being done in early childhood development, learning, and alternatives in schooling. I had heard about homeschooling, but I was not attracted to homeschooling. I am civic-oriented: I believe in public education.

When we moved up here, I started to search for a school, but no alternatives were offered. It was just very traditional schools, which in my experience were sterile and lacked color. I don't like fluorescent lights. I don't like that the kids are confined to a desk. I don't like the noise. It is just not a child-friendly environment.

Schools also herd all the kids together in one building, separate from society. My whole idea was allowing us to respond to everything in life, going here and going there, having time to talk to people, and being involved in all kinds of experiences. I don't like the term "homeschooling," because home was just our base; we were not confined to our house.

What I did was send my children to school in the morning for the social aspect and picked them up at noon. My kids were actually in public school when this whole thing first started, and I was summoned to court. I considered us a private school working with the public school. Others imposed the homeschooling definition on what I was doing. I did not consider myself "homeschooling."

When Katy was four, I went to the school to learn about kindergarten. The principal said to me, "We feel if we've got all the kids here, we need to teach them. If they just want to play, they can stay home." I have a strong philosophy of learning by playing and integrating all the learning skills you would need as they are playing store or other imaginative games. His ideal was exactly opposite what I wanted. So I skipped kindergarten.

The next year, I went to the superintendent and asked if we could just pick our kids up after lunch, because I figured they'd have socialization time at lunch. He agreed. I also had a fantasy of meeting other mothers and being in the PTA.

At that time [1980], a man in Deer River, who hadn't even graduated from high school, was homeschooling his kids and had been taken to court. He had won his case. Mr. Maertens, the superintendent, said he had been watching the case and told me, "If you want to homeschool your kids, fine with me."

He was totally open to whatever arrangement I wanted. I had excellent relationships with all the teachers, the principal, and the superintendent.

When Katy was in third grade, the teacher gave a spelling test in the morning at school, but they were doing spelling in the afternoon when Katy wasn't there. I asked the teacher, "May Katy have her schoolbook for spelling?" The teacher just peeked out of the door and said, "The superintendent told me not to give you any books."

The State Department had told Mr. Maertens to discontinue the arrangement he had with me, because there were court cases involving homeschooling taking place around the state. Every superintendent was interpreting the law their own way. There was really no rhyme or reason to how they were making those decisions.

A professor of physics in northwest Minnesota was homeschooling his child. The child had learning disabilities and had been physically abused in the school. This parent was taken to court and not allowed to homeschool.

At the same time as my case, there was a Catholic family who withdrew their kids from Catholic school to homeschool. They were taken to court. There were other cases also. I think that's why the state stepped in and said, "We can't have every school district doing their own thing."

Summons to Court
Jeanne:

In October 1983, I received a summons to court. It was the day after my birthday, and I thought, *What am I going to do?* It must have been a couple of months until the court date, because I didn't feel any panic, but I knew I had to look at my options.

The next month, the public school teachers went on strike: I didn't have the option of putting my kids in school full-time, because school wasn't open. I thought, *Well, I'll try home educating and see how they do while the schools are closed.* My kids were so attentive and interested, I thought, *Well, we'll just continue on like this.*

Public school was in session, as usual, after the Christmas holiday, but I did not return my daughters. I didn't see myself as withdrawing them from school. I had just discontinued including the public school. The arrangement hadn't fulfilled what I wanted anyway. My daughters were just meeting kids on the school bus that they knew anyway, because they were our neighbors. So it wasn't meeting the fantasy that I had of the benefits of being socially involved in the public school.

I also reflected that, if public school was important for social development, we—the majority who attends public school—would all be wonderful citizens, voting, and socially engaged; that wasn't the case. Social objectives in the education system are ideals, not reality.

I started thinking about my options and calling different sources. I was a fan of John Holt. We had his books in our library. So I called John Holt. He was very supportive of my continuing what I was doing but didn't have services to offer. I also called the Hewitt Foundation. Raymond Moore was very supportive, and he talked to me quite a bit. He volunteered to attest for me if anything happened.

My brother-in-law was close friends with John Mack, the attorney for the "Willmar 8" case [1977: women at a bank in Willmar were being demoted and having to train in their superiors]. He was interested in such cases and took our case, only charging his expenses.

Pre-Trial Hearing
Jeanne:

We had a pre-trial hearing [1984] to determine what the case was about. So, was I some kind of a criminal? What did I do? What was the charge? It was very difficult to figure out what charges were being made by the school district. "Kids are required to go to school." It didn't give any guidance at all. So the pre-trial was worthless. The attorney was discouraged. He didn't have a clear strategy on how to defend me. What was the charge? Teacher impersonation? It was just strange.

County Court Trial

Jeanne:

We went to trial. My attorney's defense was that the children were learning well, and that my teaching ability was essentially equivalent, but the judge ruled right from the start that "how well the children were learning was irrelevant." He didn't allow anything to be presented.

Raymond Moore from the Hewitt Foundation was going to testify, along with my best friend and next-door neighbor; she was a second-grade school teacher in Warba. From the time of the summons, my kids had been making books every month of their studies, but the judge ruled all of it "irrelevant." The subject was not education.

As far as being essentially equivalent, I didn't have a teaching degree, but I did have training experience. I had gone to Hamline University for two years, and I had all my training experiences through the La Leche League. The attorney also tried to show that, in the record at the time, there weren't any laws about teachers' training; only colleges had training guidelines. But we lost.

That was pretty shattering. I had a strong educational philosophy about the zest of learning and discovery. Having the court rule that irrelevant left me at a total loss as to how to defend myself.

Appeal to District Court

Jeanne:

We appealed to the district court, and this time our attorney tried a different argument. His first argument was that the children were well educated, and I was capable of teaching them. When we appealed, he argued it was my parental right to decide how to raise my children.

The court's response was that I did not have that right; it was the state's responsibility to make sure children were educated. It was very disturbing for me to hear the state say it was their right and not mine to educate my children.

I had lost again. But if I'd actually won the trial, it would have been just another homeschooling case. Another family would have been harassed, brought to trial, and who knows how they would have been treated. So, in retrospect, it was best that I lost, because we appealed to the Supreme Court.

The Minnesota Supreme Court
Jeanne:

You don't know, when you appeal, if the Minnesota Supreme Court will accept your case, but they did. My attorney was very excited about going to the supreme court. This time he argued that the law was unconstitutionally vague, because every superintendent was doing their own thing with the law. He also filed a form that allowed all of our previously rejected evidence to move on to each level. So when we went to the supreme court, it was all there.

At the same time [July 1985], the Minnesota Supreme Court heard both my case and another homeschooling case—a Catholic family from western Minnesota [the Budkes]. I listened as the two attorneys gave their oral arguments. I remember, my defense attorney said of the state, "You have this ideal of what you want, but then you're penalizing families for being responsible and raising their children."

The judges made a decision on my case first. They ruled that the law was "unconstitutionally vague"—at which point, they didn't have to make a decision on the other family's case because the initial ruling threw out the Compulsory Attendance Law.

The order from the court was that a legislative committee or task force had to be created, which was to be comprised of a variety of educators, including parents, to clarify the law.

I was emotionally wiped out by then and didn't participate, but I didn't like that the task force had an emphasis on test scores and commercially produced tests. I didn't like testing as a measure, because I felt that tests define your curriculum, your pace, and priorities. My idea was holistic: raising children to be healthy, capable, and competent people. Academics is just one part of that.

We waited for the task force and legislators to make revisions. That was months.

I did not put my kids back in public school; instead we continued with home-based education. For curriculum, I had a very general theme, and then for each year from that general theme I would pick a specific topic for each month. For example, the general theme would be winter and the topic would be Iceland. We developed our own curriculum, so all the resources we selected would tie into the topic. Everything was integrated, and my children would make books monthly of all their studies.

We had a structured time for two hours in the morning. In the afternoon, we had community activities or our daughters would make their own plans, but I would set the environment. They were very good at managing their time, and without the bell, they had longer attention spans.

When we were out places, people would always ask, "Why aren't you in school?" We'd be at an historic site and someone would say that, and I'd think, *Oh right, it would be so much better for them to be sitting at a desk.* Learning wasn't imposed on them; it was something they genuinely experienced and wanted. My aim was for them to be lifelong learners.

I do strongly believe in free public education for all, but I wish it were better with more alternatives. My dream would be that it would be clear that children's education is the parent's responsibility. I think that parents should be involved with schools and know what is going on in the schools. If they don't, I see that as child neglect.

My motive when I started alternative educating was my educational philosophy, but there were so many other benefits. I always loved it that our daughters were not regimented on how to sit—we'd be curled up in the recliner—or what to wear or limited in spontaneity. They never had to wait for their meals. They didn't get all those sicknesses. We could also schedule around my husband's shift work: all the same days he had off, we had off. I just loved the pace and integration of our lifestyle. Home-based education turned out to be so healthy.

Chapter Seven

The Newhouses start TEACH (Teaching Effective Academics at Home) and begin homeschooling their children. Connecting with MÂCHÉ, they join the MÂCHÉ board of directors. The Newhouses are also asked to participate in the Compulsory School Attendance Task Force as representatives for the private sector of education to help create the new Compulsory Attendance Law.

Interview (August 9, 2013) with:
Bob Newhouse (Founder of TEACH and Past MÂCHÉ Board Member)
> Wife: *Bethany (Past MÂCHÉ Board Member)*
> Children: *Jonathon, Jeremy, Sarah, Marija, Joseph.*

Bob:

I went to the University of Minnesota for five years but dropped out before I graduated. Instead, I went hitchhiking around the world, hoping to find God. After five years of doing this, I finally surrendered my life to Christ and was called to the mission field in Europe. I became a teacher at a Montessori school in Italy, where I met my wife, Bethany. After a couple years, we moved to Peru, where our first son, Jonathon, was born. After a couple years of mission work, we moved back to the United States.

Once we returned, I went back to college and got a degree in education, just in case I ever wanted to educate my children myself. I took my responsibilities as a father very seriously, and I didn't trust that the public education system would train-up my children in the ways of the Lord, because it certainly didn't do that for me. At the time, I never heard of anyone else homeschooling their children. After I graduated, my first teaching position was at Faith Academy in Fridley, Minnesota.

In the fall of 1982, I attended the Institute in Basic Life Principles with members of the school board. At this seminar, Mr. Gothard introduced the concept of home education. I was sitting next to the chairman of the board, and I said, "Do you think we should get involved working with homeschoolers? They believe they are called by God to do that, and they might need help. We could take them under the umbrella of Faith Academy." He said, "Bob, we don't have the finances to branch out like that." I said, "But I just sense that we should start offering services and protection to these families."

Roger Schurke and Jim Coleman were also at that seminar. During one of the breaks, Roger and Jim organized an impromptu meeting for anybody interested in homeschooling, and a couple weeks later they hosted an information meeting at Powderhorn Park in Minneapolis. I believe that was the first public meeting MÂCHÉ ever had.

A few months later, in January, Faith Academy opened an umbrella program for five homeschooling families. The next fall, twenty-nine families signed up. Enrolling at Faith Academy suddenly became quite confusing. The secretaries kept having to ask, "Which program are you in? The school or the homeschool?" Soon the school board called me in and said, "Bob, we believe God wants you to take your group of homeschoolers and split off from Faith Academy and start your own organization." I asked them, "If we're not with Faith Academy, how will I earn an income and support my family?" One said, "I guess you'll have to live by faith." I said, "Oh no. It's come to that!"

TEACH
Bob:

So, in the fall of 1983, we started T.E.A.C.H. (Teaching Effective Academics and Character at Home) and began ministering to families who felt called by God to train their children at home. The next fall, we had sixty-five families wanting to enroll. I knew I couldn't handle that many families myself, so I cried out for God's help. Within the next five days, six different teachers called me, and all asked me the same question: "We hear you're working with homeschoolers. Do you need any help?" They became our first consultants, and I began to be more confident that God was behind this.

We met a need, and our support groups were places where people could come with their struggles and get encouragement. We helped guide them academically, but, more importantly, we did a lot of family counseling and emphasized godly character. We've seen that when we focus on training children in godly character, academic excellence will follow, much like a caboose follows a train.

When my oldest son, Jonathon, turned five, we sent him to kindergarten at Faith Academy. He had an outgoing, fun-loving free spirit, but I noticed he would come home like the weight of the world was on his shoulders. I asked him, "Jonathon, what is the matter?" He said, "Papa, these kids say they are Christians, but they don't act like it." It broke my heart to see him burdened like that. Shortly thereafter we decided to bring him home and educate him ourselves. Soon my son's joy and exuberance returned. That alone was worth it to me, and I became more dedicated to the cause.

MÂCHÉ Involvement
Bob:

Shortly after the Powderhorn Park meeting in November of 1983, Jim Voeller and his family went to the Philippines to become missionaries. MÂCHÉ was looking for someone to take their place and asked if we wanted to be on the board of directors. We accepted, and my first job was to write an article for their newsletter on the father's role in homeschooling.

I remember talking to Roger Schurke one Saturday afternoon on what to call this new organization and its newsletter. Roger said, "I think we'll call it the Minnesota Association of Christian Home Educators, and the acronym will be MACHE." He pronounced it phonetically. I said, "Roger, if that's going to be the name, you could put an accent at the end and pronounce it like they do in

French, MÂCHÉ. Then we could call the newsletter *The Paper MÂCHÉ.*" Roger said, "Hey, I never thought of that. That's a great idea!"

I don't think there would be a MÂCHÉ without Roger's influence. Roger had a real heart and vision for homeschooling. When he came back from living in Washington, God used Roger to bring MÂCHÉ into existence more than anybody. He even helped us in the beginning with legal advice for turning TEACH into a nonprofit organization, for which we are very grateful.

In the spring of 1985, we had our first MÂCHÉ conference at Faith Academy. It was for one day and held in the gymnasium. I was able to borrow samples of Faith Academy's textbooks so people could see the Christian curriculum that we used. We offered to order copies through the school, because A Beka wouldn't sell textbooks directly to homeschoolers at that time.

In the fall of 1985, we had the MÂCHÉ meeting at the Edina High School. We invited the Hecker family to come sing and be our first keynote speakers. I offered to bring curriculum from Faith Academy and set up a few tables to show people samples of curriculum they could use. I also offered to contact some Christian publishers I knew and see if they would like to send representatives and curriculum to our meeting. I think only three representatives responded, but that quickly grew from there!

The third MÂCHÉ conference was at Crystal Evangelical Free Church, where I went to church, and it seemed the homeschooling movement had suddenly exploded! Many more publishers and suppliers wanted to be at the conference, and several other states began having conventions.

Shortly after, I resigned from the MÂCHÉ board. I wanted to spend more time focusing on TEACH, counseling and working with homeschooling families more intimately.

Back then, people had to have a conviction that God was calling them to homeschool, because there was a real possibility of going to jail. Those who had only a personal preference to homeschool would be unwilling to suffer that consequence. (Personally, I think that sometime in the near future, homeschoolers may have to make that decision again and consider if they are willing to suffer the consequences for their conviction to homeschool their children. I hope I am wrong.)

In that first year, one of our TEACH families was challenged by their superintendent for being truant. We met with him for an on-site visit. After he saw what they were actually doing, he said, "This family really is giving their children a good education, but we're going to bring them to court anyway." I was shocked and asked, "Why would you bring them to court if you admit they are doing a good job?" He said, "Because that's the way we're interpreting the law, which says that they must have an *equivalent* education. We don't believe this is *equivalent*." That's the kind of rigid thinking we were up against.

The Compulsory School Attendance Task Force
Bob:

So, in 1985, the law [the old compulsory attendance law] was struck down as unconstitutionally vague because the word "equivalent" was open to various interpretations. In 1986, Barry Sullivan, the assistant to the commissioner of education, Dr. Ruth Randall, called me and asked, "Would you and Bethany be interested in being on the Governor's Task Force to rewrite the Compulsory Education Law?" I said, "I don't know what we'd have to offer, but we're willing if you'd like us to." [Bob was Bethany's alternate for the task force meetings.]

Little did I know, when this task force started, nobody thought it would work. People in the legislature were saying, "You expect six private school representatives and six public school representatives to come to a consensus of what should be in this law? That'll never happen!"

The task force members representing the private schools and homeschools included Roger Schurke, from MÂCHÉ; Brother William Rhody, from the Catholic Archdiocese; Dr. Ed Johnson, from Rosemount Baptist; and a few others. I remember Ed Johnson saying in the beginning of the process, "All I want in the law is a statement that says that 'children are an heritage of the Lord.' That's the one thing I believe must be in the new statute." Our side debated, disagreed, and argued amongst ourselves for hours about what else should be on our agenda, and eventually we came to an agreement.

The six people representing the public school side operated quite differently. They spoke with one voice and were very united, but it was like they were always waiting for one particular person to voice his opinion before they'd speak. That person with the most influence was Dr. Lew Finch, the superintendent of Anoka School District, the largest school district in Minnesota.

Before the task force started, Dr. Finch went on radio, TV, and newspapers and voiced his opinion. "Anyone who home schools their children is guilty of educational child neglect." That's the kind of attitude we were up against.

I remember once Commissioner Randall asked a public school representative his opinion on a certain item on our agenda. His response was "Well, I'm not sure. I will have to think about that." She asked the next person, and she also said, "I'm not sure either. Give me a little time to ponder it." Eventually, she asked Dr. Finch, who gave his opinion on the matter, and suddenly everyone would agree with him, "Yes, that's what I think too."

This happened over and over again, and finally even Commissioner Randall asked them, "Must you all have to wait for Dr. Finch to tell you what to think?"

The bottom line is that the task force was not making progress. Months had passed, and we weren't any closer to getting a consensus than when we started.

During a break in one of the final sessions, I overheard a conversation between a father and Dr. Finch. Dr. Finch responded to him, "If you're such a concerned parent, why aren't you home, teaching your children? Why are you wasting your time here?" This man unfortunately responded back in like manner, "Well, if you're such a good superintendent, what are you doing here? Why aren't you back in your district, superintending your schools?"

Dr. Finch exclaimed in frustration, "Oh, the arrogance of you homeschoolers!" and he walked away from him.

I caught up to him and said, "Dr. Finch, what happened back there?" He looked at me and said, "Newhouse, I'm just sick and tired of being seen as an evil person," and he walked away from me too.

The meeting ended, still without the slightest bit of consensus between the two groups. We had two meetings left and, at that point, Commissioner Randall's reputation was at stake. She had to have a consensus to bring before the legislature, and the task force had nothing to offer.

One night during that week, I woke up from sleep having had a very vivid dream, which was unusual because I rarely dream at all. In this dream, I was at a task force meeting, and Dr. Finch said to me, "Newhouse, when is the last time you've been in a public school?" "Probably when I graduated." He said, "Well, they've changed a lot since then. You need to come and visit one and see what they're like now." "Okay, I'll plan on doing that sometime." He said, "Let's go now." I said, "But, Dr. Finch, it's midnight." "Come on! You said you'd be willing to go, so let's go!"

So, in the dream, we got in his car and drove to the Anoka High School in the middle of the night. As I looked in the windows I saw students playing basketball and sitting in the halls talking. The moment we entered the school, all of the students stopped what they were doing and came to greet Dr. Finch. They were all gathered around him, much like children greeting their father coming home from work. They loved and admired him, and I could see that he loved them in return.

We went to his office, and he began to earnestly tell me how much he loved these kids, and then suddenly I woke up. The dream was over. It seemed so real.

As I lay there in bed, thinking about the dream, I had the distinct impression that I was supposed to personally call Dr. Finch and tell him this dream. I said to myself, "No way! I am not going to call Dr. Finch and tell him I had a dream about him!"

So I resisted that impulse all morning. You know how it is when God is prompting you to do something that you don't want to do, and it bugs you and bugs you until you do it? Well, finally at about eleven o'clock, I said, "Okay, I'll call him already!"

I picked up the phone and dialed the number. As it rang, I thought to myself, *I hope he's not there.* The secretary answered, and I asked, "May I speak with Dr. Finch?" She said, "No, he's not here right now. Can I get your name and have him call you back?" I said, "No, it's not that important. I just wanted to know if he was in." I was about to hang up, and she said, "Oh, wait, he just walked in the door. I'll put him on." I thought, *Oh, rats! If only I would have called two minutes earlier!*

Dr. Finch picked up the phone. "Hello, who is this?" I said, "Dr. Finch, this is Bob Newhouse." "Newhouse? From the task force?" "Yes, sir." He said, "What do you want?" I thought, *How am I going to say this?* "Dr. Finch?" He said, "Yes?" I said, "Dr. Finch, umm…" He said, "Newhouse, I'm really busy right now. Tell me what you want to say." So I blurted out, "Dr. Finch, I had a dream about you last night." Before he got a chance to say anything, I told him the entire dream. At the end, I said, "Dr. Finch, I think God gave me that dream to show me your heart, and that you really do love those kids, and I want to apologize on behalf of the homeschoolers in the state and myself for seeing you as an evil person. Will you please forgive us?"

There was a long silence. Finally, I said, "Dr. Finch, are you still there?" He said, "I'm here. I heard you, and I was thinking about it, and I suppose, if there really were concerned parents who were willing to make the time and effort, they could probably do a pretty good job educating their children at home."

My jaw dropped to the desk. "Dr. Finch, I appreciate you saying that. On this task force sometimes I feel like we're just not communicating." Then I asked, "Dr. Finch, would you be willing to talk to somebody who might be able to explain this concept of home education better than I?" He said, "Who are you thinking of?" I said, "I'd like to see if I could get you to speak to Mr. Bill

Gothard." He said, "Bill Gothard? Is he the one that has that seminar with a red notebook?" I said, "Yes! Have you been to it?" He said, "No, but my wife has." I said, "Would you be willing to talk to him?" He said, "Sure. I'll talk to him if you can arrange it."

So I immediately called Bill's secretary, his sister Laura, and she said she would arrange a telephone meeting between the two men. And with that, I left it in God's hands.

The next day was the second-to-the-last task force meeting. Since this was the two-hundred-year anniversary of the Constitutional Convention, I read with my family that morning from *The Light and the Glory* by Peter Marshall, about how when they could not come to agreement on the details of what should be in the Constitution, Benjamin Franklin stood up and said, *"We need to pray. If God knows when a sparrow falls, how can we expect to raise up a nation without His assistance?"* They opened in prayer and shortly thereafter came to a consensus.

So, just before the task force meeting, I met Commissioner Randall in the hallway and read to her from that section of the book and asked, "If Benjamin Franklin could convince a deadlocked Constitutional Convention to open their session in prayer, would you consider opening this deadlocked task force meeting in prayer also?" She said, "Hmmm. Let me think about it."

I went to my seat at the table and waited for the meeting to start. Commissioner Randall came in and started the meeting by saying, "The Constitutional Convention was held two hundred years ago this month. When they could not come to a consensus as to what should be in the Constitution, Benjamin Franklin stood and suggested that they open in prayer and ask for Divine intervention. We find ourselves in a similar predicament, and I suggest that we do as they did. She asked everyone to bow their head, and she opened the session in prayer.

When she finished, she said, "We have a lot of work to get done today, because we have to present a bill to the state legislature, and we're running out of time."

Immediately Dr. Finch stood up and said, "I have something to say." Commissioner Randall said, "Lew, will you please sit down. Every time you speak there's an argument, and we don't have time for that now." He said, "Just give me five minutes." She said, "Okay, Lew, you have five minutes, but that's all!"

Dr. Finch said, "I talked to a very persuasive man yesterday who gave me a perspective I had never seen before. After much consideration, this is what I think should be in this new compulsory attendance law." He started listing his points that he wanted in the statute, and ironically, everything he said was already on our agenda.

When he finished, Commissioner Randall said in amazement, "Lew, you've made some very good points that I think we can work with!" She then asked the rest of the public school representatives, "What do you think of Dr. Finch's suggestions?" And one by one they each said, "I think it's great!" Another said, "I agree wholeheartedly!" "Brilliant!" Every one of the representatives agreed with Dr. Finch, and within ten minutes of the start of the meeting we had a consensus! It was nothing short of miraculous!

We then went before the legislature to present our bill, and I remember a certain senator saying, "Statutes do not have preambles in them. I suggest we remove this part about parents being the ones who are responsible to determine the means and methods by which their children should be educated." That was the wording that Dr. Ed Johnson wanted in the statute, and he was ready to defend it, but instead our former adversary, Dr. Finch, got to the microphone first and said, "Either take this statute in its entirety, or you will have to go back and do it all over again with a different task force, because we are all in agreement on this. Take it as it is." And eventually they did, and it became law.

It was a great bill, because it allowed freedom to homeschool with accountability. Homeschooling was now legal and under the protection of the local superintendent.

We also put in that bill that if a school was accredited and the accrediting agency's standards covered the specific requirements found in the state statute, then that school would not have to also be accountable to their local superintendent.

After the bill was made into law, Barry Sullivan encouraged us that TEACH should seek to become a recognized accrediting association. I said, "Why? We believe God gave us the concept of TEACH, and we're not going to change our program just to gain state recognition." He assured me that we wouldn't have to change anything, and if we became a recognized accrediting agency, it would mean our families would not have to be accountable to both TEACH and their local superintendent. Our families would be under our umbrella of authority, and they could then focus their time on educating their children rather than having to convince their local superintendent that they were doing a good job. So we applied for recognition to the newly formed Nonpublic Education Council, and they accepted us.

I believe the day is coming when there will be a resurgence of the battle over who owns the children. That battle was fought in 1987, and God won a major victory, which has resulted in twenty-six years of relative peace in the homeschooling arena and an entire generation of children being trained at home in the ways of the Lord. I hope and pray that TEACH will still be here to help fight that battle when it comes. No matter how intense the battle is, we must remember that we wrestle not against flesh and blood but against spiritual wickedness in high places. Our greatest weapon in this battle is the love of Christ, and that should be our central course when we educate our children at home.

Advice

Bob:

Academic knowledge is not what is going to make you successful in life. Having the character of Jesus Christ indwelling you will bring about real success and treasure in life. Therefore, focus on training your children in godly character.

If I had it to do all over again, I would love my wife more than my children. We were both so focused on raising our five children to serve God that we, in a practical sense, loved our children more than each other. Focusing on our children first prevented us from experiencing the relationship of love that Christ has for His bride, the church.

Chapter Eight

Senator Gen Olson is asked to carry homeschool legislation. She chief authors a bill and gets involved with the provisions dictating the structure of the Compulsory School Attendance Task Force that drafts a bill, which will make homeschooling legal.

Interview (January 22, 2013) with:
Senator Gen Olson (A Friend of Homeschoolers)

"In 1982, I was elected for something I never aspired to do. It was a calling."

—Gen

Gen:

Looking back on the homeschooling movement, the influence of Bill Gothard (Institute in Basic Life Principles) was very important.

I remember the first time Bill Gothard came to St. Paul, I believe in the 1970s. Here's one guy talking with an overhead projector to fifteen or twenty thousand people, and I thought, *This I have to see.* It was unbelievable; you didn't move. Everyone had these red notebooks and was taking notes. I still have mine.

I have looked back at that experience many times, and I have thought of the importance of his promotion of homeschooling when I see the trends that have been going on now with the rewriting of the standards.

The First Bill (Senate File 1696)
Gen:

The ruling came down on Jeanne Newstrom's case, which struck down our Compulsory Attendance Law, and the Schurkes, the Newhouses, and Pam von Gohren were some of the homeschoolers who were active early on with trying to create new homeschool legislation.

The reflection I made, when I was first asked to consider carrying homeschool legislation by a group of people who were working on a bill to make homeschooling legal, was "Who knows their children better than the parents? Why would they not be looking out for the best interests for their child's education?" Not all education takes place in a schoolroom.

I agreed to chief author their bill. When that bill was first presented was a memorable moment for me, because I noticed, in that committee hearing room [crowded with homeschool families], you could have heard a pin drop. It was quite obvious that there was no stress on the homeschool families to manage or control their children.

Senator Pehler also introduced a bill to study the matter and develop a proposal for requirements for being a "school." His bill included a task force to carry out this work. Though our bill was not acted upon, we were successful in amending Senator Pehler's bill to provide a framework for the task force and what we wanted them to address. Our amendment was successful and led to the task force coming back with something very similar to the bill with which we had started.

The Compulsory School Attendance Task Force
Gen:

The task force, along with its makeup, was put in law, assuring its representatives were from public schools and private schools, as well as home educators. I was not a member of the task force, but I did attend one or more of the meetings as an observer when recommendations were being formulated.

One thing I remember hearing about was Bethany Newhouse, a member of the task force. Every time the task force had a meeting, she brought loaves of fresh baked bread made by her homeschooled children for every one of the task force members. May be unfair advantage, but that's got to be impressive. It was a nice touch that I think helped soften the challenge.

Bob Newhouse shared with me a perspective that I wasn't even totally aware of, about some of the challenges. It's really almost a miracle that particular superintendent, Lew Finch, who was superintendent of Anoka-Hennepin District 11 when I was serving as secondary vocational director there, gave support and his recommendation to go forward.

Superintendent Lew Finch presented the final recommendation to the legislature. Senator Pehler, the chair of the committee, chief authored that bill, and I was a co-author.

In that legislation, one of the things we did was have a clear statement at the beginning of the Compulsory Attendance Law, which kept the focus that educating is the parent's responsibility. The state has the responsibility of providing a system of education, but they should not have control over the parents' decisions. I have been a fan of school choice of all kinds. I think home education is the ultimate choice. It may not be for everyone. It's a major decision, and I don't think people make that decision lightly.

Homeschooling is often challenged as being detrimental to a child's socialization, often raised as a weakness of homeschooling. In reality, homeschooled young people learn to be interactive and comfortable with all ages, not just a peer group.

Just this last year the Gale Woods Farm, in the Three Rivers system, had their farm breakfast. A friend and I went, and we were sitting outside on the deck. A young lady was pouring coffee. I asked her a couple of questions, and she just entered very comfortably into conversation. I don't know how it happened to come up, but it turned out she was a homeschooled student. Being able to engage personably with people is one of the soft skills a lot of employers are looking for these days.

Colleges have also recognized that homeschooling students come with better study habits and self-discipline.

It gives me a warm feeling in my heart that the efforts we have put forward are bearing fruit and that homeschooling has a quality and a magnitude, which I think makes it very difficult to discredit.

Chapter Nine

The Lindstroms choose to withdraw their children from public school and to homeschool before it's considered legal. Having been a social worker, Ruth brings an informed perspective to the Minnesota Capitol and testifies before the House and Senate on behalf of forming a new Compulsory Attendance Law that will make homeschooling legal in Minnesota. The Lindstroms start the Rochester Area Association of Christian Home Educators (RAACHE) to fellowship with and support other early homeschoolers, and they join the MÂCHÉ board of directors, where they serve in numerous capacities for fourteen years.

Interview (2011 and August 1, 2013) with:
Dean and **Ruth Lindstrom** (Past MÂCHÉ Board Members)
Children: *Sarah, David, Amy, Steven*

Ruth:

As a result of my college background, I was a deistic evolutionist. I believed that God had created the world but that He had used evolutionary techniques to do it. One evening, needing a night out but short of money, Dean and I decided to attend a lecture at a Mayo Clinic presentation hall. The lecturer, using scientific evidence and mathematical data, made a convincing argument that there had to have been a specific creation and that this was a young earth. I was riveted. The lecturer was Dr. Henry Morris. It was a life-changing event for me and for Dean.

A few months later, Dr. Francis Schaeffer came to the Mayo Clinic, and we were involved in the first showing of "How Shall We Then Live." It was right up my field of humanities, and I remember saying to Dean, "We have been brainwashed by our wonderful liberal education! This is certainly a different perspective on history." We had no idea about homeschooling at that point in our life, but I began to have a growing dread of the day we would have to put our children in school.

We entered Sarah, our oldest, in a bilingual nursery school when she turned three. Sarah loved it. Unfortunately, by the second year we began to see some alarming changes. Sarah would contradict and refuse to do things with "But my teacher says..." or "But the other kids don't do it this way." She was becoming more and more like a little rebellious teenager. It must have been the Spirit of God that gave me the good sense to realize that if she was going to be like this as a preschooler, we'd lost her already.

We took Sarah out of preschool. It was the best thing we could have done for her. I had a background in social work, but no one had, or was, talking about the negative impact of school socialization. Having those early experiences and insights from God helped me to formulate my own insights and realizations that the best socialization occurs in the family—the most basic social institution created by God for our good.

We kept Sarah home from school two extra years until we couldn't put it off any longer. We thought conventional schooling was something we had to do. We didn't realize there was any other way. The first morning Sarah was at school, I cried. I couldn't stop crying. My sister called, and I remember saying, "What's wrong with me? Why can't I get over this separation anxiety?"

My sister said, "It's perfectly normal." She then said, "I just heard a man on the Phil Donahue Show. I think his name was . . . ummm, Dr. Raymond Moore. He doesn't think anybody should send their kids to school until they're at least nine or eleven."

I tried to dismiss it. It seemed preposterous, but the idea that somebody thought kids shouldn't start school until nine or maybe even eleven years of age stayed in the back of my mind. That was 1979, the year Steven, our youngest child, was born. Over the next couple years, I read the two books in which Dr. Moore recommends later entry into classrooms. His conclusions, based on research I was familiar with, made a great deal of sense to me.

By the summer of 1982, I was becoming more and more convicted about homeschooling. I prayed that if we were supposed to do this "bizarre" thing, Dean would change his mind and be willing.

I also prayed, "Lord, if we're supposed to homeschool, please get us in touch with people who are homeschooling." That summer, my sister said, "I know someone who is homeschooling. Their name is Coleman." She got me in touch, and I went to the Coleman's home and spent an afternoon with them. That was very helpful.

In the spring of 1983, our children were still in public school and I was very active there. As a Christian, I wanted to be "salt and light." I was a room mother and on the PTA board of directors, so I knew the administrators and teachers well. But some things troubled me.

Reasons for Homeschooling
Ruth:

David, our second born, loved numbers and arithmetic. At the supper table, David thought it was fun to do division and multiplication with his daddy, while at school he was bored because there was no challenge. I talked to the school. They tested him and the psychologist recommended he have more challenging arithmetic. Instead, the school gave him two to three times as many of the same simple worksheets the rest of the class was doing. It was disappointing to see him "hating" school.

For a PTA meeting for parents, the teachers voted to do a program on the dangers of television. Off the record, some of the teachers said, "I wish we could just recommend eliminating TV, because it's destroying children's attention span." While our family had gotten rid of our television, the consensus at school was that few, if any, parents would be willing to do something so drastic.

There were other things that happened, but the final wake-up call for me was when Sarah was in third grade. I visited her classroom at Halloween, and I saw a number of books on witchcraft sitting on the windowsills. I was quite alarmed.

At a family camp the previous summer, a man who had been heavily demonized had given his testimony that he had had to have demons cast out of him before he could accept Christ into his life. He said as a teenager he was approached with the idea of Wicca and got involved with witchcraft in order to gain power over classmates. Here, several months later, in the fall of 1982, I walked into our daughter's classroom and saw witchcraft being promoted.

When I asked about the books, the teacher sparkled with pride and said, "That's my reading incentive program. The kids can only read them in class when they get their work done. It's an incentive because they really like reading these books. Then they write a book report and it goes in their file." I said, "Do parents get to see this file?" "Oh, no, it's just their personal file." I was horrified, and I tried to tell this teacher why it bothered me. She thought I was "wacko," that there was nothing to it. That was the final straw.

We endured the rest of the year and tried to do damage control after school each day. We never dreamed at that time in history that homeschoolers would later be able to just take their kids out after Christmas—or any other time of year. We didn't consider that option because it was considered illegal. Our children would have been considered truants, and we, their parents, accused of educational neglect. The children could have been removed from us by Social Services.

In the spring of 1983, we made the final decision to educate our children at home. A week before school was out, I went in and talked to the administrator of our school. These were colleagues I had been working with. I didn't feel it would be right to just disappear without letting them know. The administrator was furious.

At this point in history, many parents were taking their kids out and putting them into Christian schools because of prayer and Bible reading having been taken out of the schools. I tried to explain my deep concern over the schools becoming academies for teaching humanism.

My administrator refused to understand. I remember him saying as he ushered me out, "Mrs. Lindstrom, it's because of people like you, taking the good children out of school, that we're having so much trouble." He tried to tell me what a good experience public school was and how good it was for my children. As we walked out into the main office, we found a young boy weeping. It was our son David. He had brought money to pay for a lost library book that morning. Somebody had stolen the money from his backpack. Was this one of the "good" experiences my kids needed?

On the last day of school, Sarah's second-grade teacher commended us on our ability to homeschool but then, with a sincerely worried frown, asked, "But, Mrs. Lindstrom, what about your children's socialization needs?" I remember feeling like I had been stabbed. I was worried too! How were they going to develop social skills?

Legal Concerns

Ruth:

In August 1983, before we actually started homeschooling, Dean said, "Before we start, I think we need to check with an attorney." There was no Home School Legal Defense Association or MÂCHÉ yet.

We called a good friend of ours who was an attorney—we didn't know Roger Schurke—to find out what kind of legal ground we were standing on. He'd never heard of homeschooling and found the whole idea fascinating. His response was "I have a good friend in the Cities who's a constitutional attorney. You should check with him." So I did.

The constitutional attorney I called was very polite but kept probing me, "Why are you doing this?" I went through my concerns about humanism, evolution, and false worldviews being taught, etc. Finally he said, "Mrs. Lindstrom, are you doing this for religious reasons?" I said, "I guess you could say so." He responded with an emphatic "Great! We're looking for a family like yours to take through the court system to prove the law in Minnesota is unconstitutional." No one can begin to comprehend how frightening that thought was to me!

Thankfully, we didn't end up having to go through the court system, but two other families did. As a result, in 1985, the Minnesota State Supreme Court handed down the decision that the Compulsory Attendance Law in Minnesota was unconstitutionally vague, and the state legislature was mandated to readdress the law and come up with a solution in two years. And thus began a kind of "baptism by fire" for me.

The First Bill (Senate File 1696)
Ruth:

I had never been politically active, but I am concerned by nature about what is true and right, and about doing the right thing. Somehow I got involved. It must have been the Spirit of God.

The first year I worked mostly on the Senate side and got to know Senator Gen Olson, the chief author of the bill we felt was most amenable to our concerns as homeschoolers.

It was also during this time that I became acquainted with Roger Schurke. Invited to a think tank session with him and other concerned parties to scrutinize the bill, the only contribution I remember making was to point out that it would be a violation of our constitutional rights to be required to let a public official search our private homes without a court-ordered search warrant. So they changed the wording in that original provision.

When the bill finally came up in the Senate Education Committee, I remember sitting in a very crowded conference room at the State Capitol. Virtually everybody who was homeschooling in Minnesota had come for that hearing. We were fighting for our children and their future. To make room for the adults, we had all our children sit on the floor. The kids were polite, and everyone was dressed nicely.

Toward the end of the morning, one of the senators kept talking, and talking, and talking, on and on. I wondered, *Am I coming down with a migraine? I don't understand a word he's saying.*

All of a sudden I heard a *click, click, click* down the marble hall as one more senator arrived, Senator Ember Reichgott. Later I realized that Senator Pehler, the chairman, and his coalition had been taking up time, waiting for the vote needed to defeat the bill. We homeschoolers were stunned.

The committee members who had voted against us looked uncomfortable as they hurried to pick up their papers and leave. Senator Pehler broke the silence by clearing his throat uncomfortably, looking around at us families and commenting, "Well, I must commend you and your families for being so well behaved." That was the first year, 1986.

The Compulsory School Attendance Task Force
Ruth:

During the 1986-1987 school year, the work started all over on a second draft to amend the Compulsory Education Bill. The commissioner of education put together a coalition of representatives from vested educational groups. Roger Schurke and Bethany Newhouse were selected to represent home educators, but a number of us continued working behind the scenes with advice and lobbying efforts. As I look back on those two years, I am especially struck with Roger Schurke's sacrificial leadership.

Preparing to Testify
Ruth:

I had the opportunity to testify regarding the necessity of these amendments to be made in both the House and the Senate. The first testimony I offered was in the House. Nobody had asked me to testify. I just had a strong sense that I should be prepared. I remember thinking, *Okay, Lord, how am I supposed to prepare?*

As a result, I made an appointment with our county attorney— who I knew well from my days as a child protection social worker—to obtain a copy of the Child Welfare Code, which covered the statutes relating to child neglect and abuse. While letting me know he thought I was crazy to be homeschooling, he arranged for me to obtain the sections of the law I wanted in order to prepare my testimony.

House Education Committee (H.F. 432)
Ruth:

At the House Education Committee that winter, there were too many people for everyone to testify, so when the chairman called the superintendent of the Anoka School District to testify, he also commented that there would only be time for one more person to speak before the committee would begin discussion. The superintendent of Anoka Schools was adamantly opposed to homeschooling and claimed that passing such a bill would allow and perpetuate child abuse and child neglect. We homeschoolers were appalled.

There was a slight pause while the chairman reviewed his list of potential speakers, and then he called for "a Mrs. Ruth Lindstrom to speak." As I walked to the podium, committee members were shuffling papers, trying to get things tied up. They did not look like they wanted to welcome one more speaker. I was so scared. My knees were buckling, and my mouth was so dry it felt like it was packed with cotton. I breathed, "Oh, God, help me!" Then I took my reading glasses, put them on, cleared my throat, and began speaking.

My brother, who was in the audience, said, "When you put those glasses on, everyone suddenly started paying total attention." I don't remember exactly what I said, but I do remember holding up the statutes I'd gotten and saying, "This is the Child Welfare Code. This is not what we need. Home education and child protection are two separate issues." It was one of those moments where you feel like you're in a movie or something.

Senate Education Committee
Ruth:

Well, lest you think too much of me, let me tell you what happened next. Because I did such a fantastic job and everyone was so impressed with Ruth Lindstrom, they had me testify at the Senate Education Committee, too. It was a total flop.

In fact, it was one of my most embarrassing moments. The chairman of this committee had me come up first even though the senators weren't all there yet and no one seemed ready. Nobody paid any attention to anything I said. It was awful. [*She laughs*] But, the bill [making homeschooling legal] passed.

Governor Perpich signing the Compulsory
Attendance Bill into law in 1987.

During the Fight for "The Law of 1987"
Ruth:

There were so many things that happened, not only at those particular meetings, but behind the scenes. The Lord's hand was definitely on us.

The first few times going back and forth from St. Paul with all the kids in the car, I thought, *What an opportunity the Lord is giving us to teach the kids firsthand how our constitutional democratic system works and how wonderful it is.* I was learning along with them, because I didn't know how it worked. But when those first trips turned into trip after trip, I got discouraged.

One evening I especially remember. I was so tired! I remember fighting tears—as well as traffic—on the way home and asking the Lord, "How long am I going to have to do this?" I was listening to KTIS when all of a sudden an anthem came on. I don't remember what it was, but it was like the voice of God speaking to me, comforting me, letting me know He was with us.

Another day I remember walking up the stairs into the Capitol with Wayne Olhoft, the director of the Berean League [the organization that became the Minnesota Family Council], and saying, "How can we ever win this? We don't have any money. We're a bunch of nobodies. We don't know what we're doing. And—" Wayne stopped stock still and somewhat fiercely said, "Ruth, never underestimate the power of being right!"

That statement has often come back to me at times when I have had to have courage to take a stand, even though in the minority.

Wayne was also the one who pointed out the quote of Jefferson's to the side of one of the chambers at the Minnesota State Capitol. "Eternal vigilance is the price of freedom." These are two important principles this next generation of homeschooling parents need to remember.

Before Homeschooling Becomes Legal
Ruth:

Having been a social worker, I was acutely aware of how easy it is to remove children from the custody of parents. Before the Compulsory Education Law was changed in 1987, my biggest fear as a home-educating mother was having the children removed from our custody.

At that point, the average time a child remained in foster care was eighteen months. Parents accused of child abuse or neglect are stripped of their constitutional rights in our juvenile code. They are considered guilty until they are proven innocent, and that's backward. You can go through a lot of heartache, and a lot of things can happen to your kids in eighteen months.

We had a plan. Because I knew if a social worker came they would have to go back and get a search order before I would let them into our home, and that would take time—at least an hour depending on how busy the judge was. So my instructions to the children were, if the doorbell rang and I gave them a sign, they were supposed to hide. Our children were to stay hidden until I rang the bell that was out on the patio. Then our plan was that I would take the kids and flee to Wisconsin. Dean would deal with the authorities and possible jail time.

Today it is hard to believe that we were that desperate. Fortunately, we never had to carry out our plan, but there were homeschoolers that had to go through similar scenarios and even face arrest in front of their children during those years.

One morning before the law was changed, our devotions were about Daniel praying and subsequently being thrown to the lions. After Dean left for work, I asked the kids, "Why do you suppose Daniel prayed out loud? Why didn't he just pray quietly so that nobody would hear him? Why did he open his window so people could hear him praying?" Then I asked, "Did you know we're breaking the law by homeschooling?"

David exclaimed, his clear blue eyes opened wide with disbelief and horror, "Mom, what in the world are we doing it for then?" I explained to the children that there are some times that we have to obey God instead of "Caesar" if God's laws supersede what "Caesar" is telling us to do. It made a powerful impact on them, because they knew their dad tried to not even break speed laws.

In 1985, when the court threw the law out, we were under no restrictions but still could have been charged with neglect, because it wasn't "legal" to homeschool either. As a result, I wouldn't let the kids play outdoors during school hours. Even after the law was passed, I was reluctant to let the kids play outdoors or to go shopping during the day.

Wanting to Give Up
Ruth:

Were there times I wanted to give up? Yes. But every time I would stop and think, I'd realize, "No, we can't go back, because someday we're going to have to answer to God about how we raised our children."

Whether it's public, private, or homeschooling, parents are going to have to answer to God about how they sought to raise their children. We have the responsibility to raise our children according to how the Lord leads us. It has to be grounded in His Word, because if we just rely on feelings, we're lost. We have to be people of the Word.

Their First Day of School
Ruth:

When we started homeschooling, my mother-in-law and father-in-law were there. They were not only opposed to homeschooling, but I had always found it tense when they were with us because I wanted them to feel I was a good wife and mother.

Further, much to our surprise, we had discovered the Christian textbook companies were unwilling to sell books to us (because we were not considered "legal" schools), and we were not able to obtain books until later that fall.

We had bought some little desks and set up a mini schoolroom downstairs. I thought, *We'll start the day with the Pledge of Allegiance, "The Star-Spangled Banner," and prayer.* Immediately I made a faux pas; I got part way through the Pledge of Allegiance and couldn't remember for sure how it went. [*She laughs*] I hoped Grandma wasn't listening too closely. I had the music for "The Star-Spangled Banner," so that wasn't quite so bad. Then I opened the day in prayer.

Grandma took pictures, and I pretended I knew what I was doing. That was our first day of school. My, how things changed as my husband and I grew and learned with our children over the years.

Starting RAACHE
Ruth:

The next semester, those of us who were homeschooling got together every month to let our kids play together while we exchanged ideas and encouraged each other. There were four of us families. That was how RAACHE [Rochester Area Association of Christian Home Educators] started.

The following year those families were either no longer in the area or no longer homeschooling, but we contacted and invited everyone else we learned about via the grapevine in southeastern

Minnesota. The support group grew, and I administrated it. We knew nothing about MÂCHÉ. When we met with Colemans, I think MÂCHÉ was just a little support group at that point.

MÂCHÉ Involvement

Ruth:

As soon as we learned that Schurkes were trying to get a statewide group going, we got a carload to go up with us. The first conference we went to, I think, was at Crystal Free Church. It was small and informal. Some of the people were very educated and others weren't. We were truly a bunch of "ragtag" people.

We got to know John and Lynne Cooke when they stayed overnight with a group of teens from the Twin Cities on a field trip to Rochester. Later, John Cooke asked us several times if we would like to go to some national conferences with them. Looking back we wonder, was he hinting at us coming on the board? We were too busy with our family, church responsibilities, work, and RAACHE to stop and consider it.

Joining the MÂCHÉ Board of Directors

Dean:

Our two oldest children participated in the MÂCHÉ graduations. Those were additional contacts with the MÂCHÉ board. My impression was that John Cooke was carrying a lot of the weight for MÂCHÉ. He was doing the newsletter. He was treasurer and conference coordinator. When we did get involved on the MÂCHÉ board in 1995, one of our first assignments was for Ruth to take over the newsletter.

Ruth:

The format of the newsletter changed when John took it over, and then I expanded it when I took it over. I remember praying, "Lord, what in the world am I supposed to do with this newsletter? What is the focus supposed to be?" I decided I should focus on our state, utilize "home grown" contributions, and make it more of an interaction with people in Minnesota.

I couldn't believe all of the thank-you notes people sent. I made some big changes, and it changed even more after I left. It's now a magazine format.

Dean:

I became the MÂCHÉ treasurer and had to be at board meetings, and I remember late nights after meetings, driving back to Rochester, and trying to stay awake.

Ruth:

It seemed like we could never get home before 2:00 a.m. We usually met in Cooke's living room. Lynne was a gracious hostess and John a good chairman. We missed them when they left the board.

I'm moved when I think of the Schurkes. Though, there were times that I felt ready to strangle Roger because I didn't like the way he conducted board meetings. He was so . . . "Roger, you were so loose." [*She laughs*]

I am an organizer. I wanted everyone to have an agenda and to submit written reports ahead of time so that we could know where we were going. I guess the Lord chose Roger partly because he was so unconventional. I'll never forget the board meeting he led while lying flat on his back, on the floor (he had back problems), with his feet up on the table in a hotel. I couldn't believe it!

But the Lord used Roger and Merryl. Merryl would keep us organized with a gentle and quiet spirit. Roger and Merryl are a man and woman deserving of honor.

Memories from MÂCHÉ

Dean:

In 1996, the MÂCHÉ conferences grew to the point they could no longer meet in churches, and so they started meeting in civic centers.

Ruth:

The growth was amazing. One of my dreams was to get more of a connection with the support groups throughout Minnesota. Pam von Gohren and later Bryants were willing to take on that responsibility, and so that was how the support group conferences started.

My favorite conference was when Jessica Hulcy and Mark Hamby were the keynote speakers—that was the first time MÂCHÉ was in Rochester [2001]. It was a good feeling for me because I had been lobbying the board for years to have it in Rochester.

Initially, people were worried we'd lose our base in the Twin Cities if we tried to meet elsewhere. The reason St. Paul, Rochester, and Duluth were eventually selected is simply because there were no other convention sites where we could fit. The problems were that a large convention room was needed along with an exhibit arena, food court, and many small breakout rooms for an affordable price.

Dean:

St. Cloud was ideally central, but it didn't have a facility that met our needs. Duluth was actually the best facility in the state. The first year we went to Rochester was because of a conflict of date or something in the Twin Cities. I don't remember exactly what it was, but that year we had to go somewhere other than St. Paul for the first time.

Ruth:

It was so nice in Rochester. Those of us on the board were treated like princes and princesses. For example, when we went to our hotel rooms the first night, we found big baskets of stuff from the Rochester Visitor and Convention Bureau to welcome us. It was quite an eye-opener to realize how important a conference like ours was to local businesses.

Dean:

A favorite story of mine from those years is the one about "the MÂCHÉ boiler." While I was treasurer, I got a letter in the mail from the State of Minnesota in which we were informed that we were negligent about having our boiler inspected at our office. MÂCHÉ didn't [and still doesn't] have an office.

Ruth:

Kitchen tables were our office, and living rooms and restaurants our board rooms.

Dean:

I wrote a letter to them and explained that we didn't have any office. It didn't matter. They kept sending us warnings. Finally, I got through to somebody, but on the board we had quite a bit of humor about our negligence with our boiler.

Other MÂCHÉ People

Dean:

I don't know how MÂCHÉ ever got along without Doris Wetjen!

Ruth:

Doris provided a tremendous relief for a lot of things that needed doing. She helped pick up things that were overwhelming us as a working board of volunteers. For example, our website.

Jerry von Gohren designed our first website. After they left, the responsibility somehow fell to me—of all people! It was not my cup of tea, and it was hard. I had to get people's input not only on the newsletter and the e-newsletter but also for the website and the handbook along with a number of other services we initiated. Thankfully, our son David worked with me as our webmaster during those years when internet communication was becoming so imperative and before Doris began helping as a contractor.

When I look back at those years, I wonder, "How did we do it all?" We were so stretched! But the Lord was good to us and helped us. It was a privilege to be part of something which was so important, and an honor to work with people like the Schurkes, Cookes, and Watkinses.

Advice

Ruth:

The Lord wants our worship. He wants us to love Him with all our heart, soul, mind, and strength. I had grown up with the idea that somehow our service was so important to the Lord, but He doesn't need our service. He owns the cattle on a thousand hills. He is sovereign. He can do anything He wants. It is simply our privilege to serve Him. It was a great privilege to serve Him by being on the MÂCHÉ board and to find that with His help I could do things I never dreamed of doing on my own.

It was also my privilege to serve the Lord by teaching and training my children with His help. It was the hardest undertaking of my life, but if I could, I would do it all over again.

It's not the curriculum. It's being faithful to the Lord and His Word that is important as we teach our children "precept upon precept and line upon line." If we can take credit for anything, it's obeying the Lord in what He has called us to do, but it is only by His grace that we could, and can, even obey Him.

Dean:

One thing I guess we probably learned is more about God's grace. When a child who has had a good, apparently spiritual upbringing, is away from the Lord you can't make any assumptions about the parents' fault. We can't take credit for any success either. We can only be thankful. It's God's grace.

Chapter Ten

The Solums start homeschooling with a group before it's legal and begin lobbying for legislation that would make homeschooling legal in Minnesota. They talk to legislators, participate in hearings, and are present when the new bill is passed and becomes law in 1987.

Written Contribution Submitted (November 22, 2013) by:
Karl and **Suzanne Solum** (Homeschool Pioneers)
Children: *Joseph, Seth, Jared, Nathan, Ethan*

Suzanne:

Looking back, it is so clear to us that it was God alone who gave His people strength, courage, and the grace to take the actions needed to bring forth homeschool education in Minnesota and across the country. He is the one we honor!

When we first started homeschooling in 1982, it was considered illegal to homeschool. Spring Grove Public School took one of the families of our Christian fellowship to court and charged them with truancy—we schooled as a group.

At that time, we decided as a fellowship to bring the superintendent and principal of Spring Grove to a few of the homes to show them the curriculum and prove the children were being educated and were well socialized. We also talked to them about our Christian convictions that led us to choose home education.

An attorney was hired to defend the family. On the basis of religious liberty, they won the case, which was watched by other counties because of all the people starting to homeschool. During this time, there were people in the country who had been put in jail for choosing to homeschool. There were no state laws at this time, so everyone who homeschooled was considered truant. People counted the cost before taking the step to home educate.

The Law of 1987
Suzanne:

At that time, we joined Home School Legal Defense Association and Christian Liberty Academy, who both encouraged us and other Christians in Minnesota to lobby our state legislature for a homeschool bill that would make it legal to homeschool with the least possible restrictions.

Karl and his brother John were both at the Capitol at different times, talking personally to as many senators and representatives as they could, describing what homeschooling was, and making a case for its legitimacy, especially in regard to our Christian convictions. They got to know other homeschoolers from around the state, including Ruth Lindstrom, who were also at the Capitol for the same purpose.

Surprisingly to us, being conservatives, we found that the Democratic senators and representatives were more helpful on the whole. There was one Christian lady—a Republican, Gen Olson—who helped and even sponsored the bill, along with some other Christian representatives. As a result, there were several hearings held where we and Christian homeschool parents from around the state testified.

Chris Klicka from Home School Legal Defense Association, Mike McHugh from Christian Liberty Academy, and Roger Schurke, a Christian attorney and one of the founders of MÂCHÉ, testified on behalf of this bill.

There was a lot of effort to put restrictions in the bill [H.F. 432], making it impossible for parents to teach, but because of the organizations HSLDA, MÂCHÉ, CLA, and others who could show proof of how well homeschoolers were doing without restrictions, a bill was passed that enabled parents to teach their children at home with very few restrictions.

We will never forget when one of the representatives said to us, "Tell us what you want. We are not your sovereigns." We had made the point countless times that we were not asking permission from the state to give our children a Christian education; rather it was a God-given responsibility to parents and a right under our Constitution: the First and Fourteenth Amendments. A key point that was emphasized and finally legally recognized was that it is the parents' job to teach their children themselves or delegate the responsibility to whomever they chose, whether public or private or home education. The state may only step in when it has been proven that the parents are failing in their responsibility.

It is fun thinking back about all we went through, and how blessed we were to give our children a Christian homeschool education!

Chapter Eleven

John Tuma is a lawyer and, since 2003, has also volunteered as MÂCHÉ's legislative liaison. He and his wife Wendy are current members of the MÂCHÉ board of directors. John gives his perspective of the bill that was passed into law in 1987.

Interview (December 1, 2012) with:
John Tuma (MÂCHÉ's Legislative Liaison and MÂCHÉ Board Member)
> Wife: *Wendy (MÂCHÉ Board Member)*
> Children: *Cal, Molly*

The Homeschool Law of 1987
John:

Roger Schurke created a law [while working on the task force] that was really convoluted and almost impossible to understand, or he at least advocated for all of these little nuances. It really was masterful.

When you look at the nuances and the twists and turns of the law, it looked as if he was giving something to the school districts, but the reality was he wasn't giving them anything. We could have twisted it in any way we wanted.

It was really brilliant, but I think there were a lot of homeschoolers who just wanted it to say, "Homeschooling is absolutely, without a doubt, unquestionably legal. Leave us alone." You also had the people who wanted to simply be accredited. Instead, Roger included things like reports and testing, and he made sure there wasn't any language about giving the testing results to the school district.

There were homeschoolers who thought MÂCHÉ was selling out and giving up too much. "We should fight this more in the courts." But Roger was smart and already knew what liberal Justice Wahl [from the Newstrom case] had pretty much said: "Yoder ain't going nowhere."

Roger knew we were going to lose if we tried to establish a win under the Federal Constitution, because the Minnesota courts weren't buying Yoder [Appendix A, V.] or the Sisters [Appendix A, II.]. We'd won by referencing the State Constitution's stand that the people of a state have to easily understand a law to be accountable enough to that law to be charged with criminally disobeying it. Therefore, the law on homeschooling was declared unconstitutionally vague.

Our next run wasn't going to be so good. We needed to work this out. So, in 1987, they compromised, and some homeschoolers showed up, saying, "This is awful" and "You are selling us out." They testified in front of the legislature, which I really don't think hurt us, because it made Roger look more reasonable.

Gen Olson was a freshman senator, very well liked, very nice person. She took over what would be considered a prestigious Republican seat and was going to be there for a while. Gen was a leading voice on bringing that bill forward. She was in the minority—someone else carried it—but she was instrumental in saying homeschooling is legitimate.

In 1987, the law [H.F 432] was adopted and homeschooling became legal. We always referred to it as "The Law in 1987." It was signed by a Democratic governor and a Democratic legislature. It was a good feat getting that passed.

There were still things like report cards and superintendent visits, which were always a pain. Roger put in there you could give them your curriculum, but the superintendent could still come and make your lives miserable if they chose. Most did not. If a superintendent asked for your curriculum, Roger had the idea of the "wheelbarrow approach." You throw all of your books in a wheelbarrow, drop it off, and say, "I want it back in a week." They will never look at it; they'll just give it back to you.

Chapter Twelve

The Cookes choose to home educate their children while it is not yet considered legal. They join the MÂCHÉ board of directors, and they and their children become very involved at MÂCHÉ conferences. John becomes the chairman of MÂCHÉ's working board, the MÂCHÉ conference coordinator, and through MÂCHÉ they make many connections to homeschoolers around the state and also with other state boards.

Interview (January 22, 2013) with:
John and **Lynne Cooke** (Past MÂCHÉ Board Members and Past MÂCHÉ Chairman)
Children: *Christine, Alan, Heidi*

John:

I was chairman of the board of Powderhorn Christian School, which originally was kindergarten through ninth grade. We had up to twelfth grade for a couple of years and had forty-five students in high school. When twenty-two of them moved to Tennessee with a church group, our family needed to decide what to do, as it was necessary to close the high school.

There was this family, Jim and Pam Coleman, whose daughter had been in our daughter's class, and they had begun to homeschool. We looked into it, and I felt that was the way we were supposed to go.

At the Christian school, we developed a home education program, where a teacher was willing to do the testing and have monthly meetings for parents who had questions.

We wrote a letter to the Minneapolis school superintendent, which laid out all of our reasons for choosing to homeschool, and began home educating in 1984. Christy was a junior, Alan was a sophomore, and Heidi would have been in fifth grade.

Lynne:

I cried a lot the first year [*she laughs*]. I did. It was totally different. I said, "Oh, Lord, why? Why at this point in my life?" The kids had been in a Christian school for a long time, and suddenly everything changed.

Change is not always easy. They were home all the time, and I felt inadequate and unprepared, but John did some of the classes with the kids. The fact that the kids were older also, in some ways, made it easier because they could do a lot themselves.

John:

After 1976, I was a self-employed consulting engineer, so that gave me greater flexibility. I could work different hours.

We would assign each of our children a subject to teach the family. I remember Alan said, "Okay, I'm the teacher, and if you want to ask a question, you have to raise your hand. That means you too, Mom and Dad." It was interesting to get the kids' different perspectives—very enjoyable.

We had flexibility and were able to do a variety of different activities you normally wouldn't do, even just the opportunity to make changes in the structure of the curriculum. I wouldn't necessarily do English, science, math, and each subject every day. We sometimes focused a week or two weeks on math and very little else. Then we'd focus on other subjects again. That was a big advantage.

We made several trips to Wisconsin. We called them family service trips. We helped my aunt and uncle move three different times, right down to the point of making sure their beds were set up and made and there was food to eat.

Lynne:

When we started, homeschooling was fairly new. We didn't see or even know what the benefits would be in the long run. I look back now and see that the children would have benefited from starting homeschooling earlier.

Even though the kids went to a good Christian school, there are other influences, dynamics, and interactions that may not be the best in any school situation regardless of whether it's Christian or not.

John:

One of the big things I see in home education is it's not a grade-level structure. It's a family structure. We'd go roller-skating sometimes with different homeschool families, and it was always interesting to see the older kids helping the younger ones—a high school kid teaching a second grader how to roller-skate. It happened in various activities. We saw that home educating helped each of our family members be individuals yet also be interrelated.

Lynne:

It was good to be together and to talk. Over meals we would sit at the table and talk, and the neighbor kids would be waiting on our front steps for our children to come out, and they'd ask, "What do you talk about for so long?"

John:

It was also good in spiritual areas. We'd spend time searching Scriptures and having different children share what they saw and their insights from different portions of Scripture. Seeing the kids mature in various ways and having the opportunity to see and encourage that was such a blessing. Rather than a teacher at a school, you are part of that process, and you see them develop.

Lynne:

Another benefit was opportunities to volunteer. Heidi volunteered at a nursing home, and they gave training sessions in how to deal with people who'd had a stroke or memory loss. That was very helpful because when my dad had his stroke, I'd take my mother out, and Heidi would stay with Grandpa. One day, he said to her, "Now, Heidi, how is it? Am I taking care of you, or are you taking care of me?" She'd say, "Grandpa, we're taking care of each other."

It was good. Interacting with the older generation I think is so important, because kids can get so busy that they don't do that. They don't realize the value, how short life really is, and how important those relationships can be.

Joining the MÂCHÉ Board of Directors

John:

A year after we began homeschooling, we were asked by Roger and Merryl Schurke to join [in 1985] the board of MÂCHÉ. Roger was chairman at that time. Prior to that, we had gone to MÂCHÉ meetings. Back then, there were two conferences a year, a spring conference and a fall conference. They were smaller, probably two to three hundred people. Bob and Bethany Newhouse were on the board then, and the Smiths, the Biedermans, and another couple. Our two youngest children were also involved in MÂCHÉ.

Lynne:

They worked at the conferences and put in a lot of time. A lot of the board members' children did. Our son actually directed the youth workers for a number of years. He always enjoyed that, and he continued on for a number of years after he graduated from high school.

John:

Christine, our oldest, was part of MÂCHÉ's first graduation ceremony in 1986. There were six graduates total: four girls and two boys.

1987 2nd MÂCHÉ Graduation: Tammi Berg, Christina Cram, Linnea Loos, Christina Kiffmeyer, Michael Marquardt, Alan Cooke

A Working Board
John:

MÂCHÉ became our life, just about. It was a working board. Through the years people would pressure us to open an office somewhere, but our goal wasn't to man an office; it was to develop the organization to help people.

One year, when I was chairman, I had all the board members keep track of the hours they spent on each different function. At the end of the year, Lynne and I had over two thousand hours. MÂCHÉ paid board members a small amount per meeting to cover fuel costs, because people came from different parts of the state.

Lynne:

That money also was used if you had to have a babysitter.

John:

Also, rather than putting money into an office, we tried to develop some equipment in each home. If someone didn't have a modem, we made sure they had one so they could do things online for us.

Some Favorite Memories
John:

Some people at MÂCHÉ will still remember this: Roger and Merryl frequently had a night class at Northwestern College on homeschooling. I would do the session on socialization. One day I took our youngest daughter with me, and I talked about how tremendous home educating is and how it develops people skills.

Heidi was standing kind of to my side, sideways, and looking down, like she was very shy. You could see people watching her, like "What's with this girl?" Then all of a sudden she turned and started sharing with them. I guess that impacted people.

One special memory was an overnight in Rochester with the Rochester support group. Ruth Lindstrom's mother was an amazing storyteller. All of us were sitting around their family room engrossed in a story. I remember looking around at everybody, from adults to the youngest, totally enraptured as she told the story.

Curriculum
John:

Nowadays, there are so many materials, which in some ways can be a detriment. Parents get too caught up and rely too much on the curriculum and not enough on developing relationships and diligently seeking the Lord as to what is important to impart.

Definitely, we need to learn to do the basics: solid reading, writing, and math skills—but are we really evaluating whether the materials are in agreement with the Scriptures and with moral values? What we saw was we needed to develop our children to be able to stand alone, to really stand for their values.

National Homeschool Meetings
John:

As a MÂCHÉ board, we were always the oldest board at every national meeting. We were the old folks. Together we had probably a couple hundred years of experience. It was interesting relating with certain state board members when the values of the boards were different. Some state boards seemed like they'd come back and their whole board would have quit over the year, and you'd just grieve.

Another thing we've seen over the years is a change in attitude, taking home educating for granted and not really understanding the things people went through in the past.

We're invited back to the MÂCHÉ conference every year, and we enjoy it. We are seeing the children of families we knew, now home educating their children, which is tremendous.

MÂCHÉ Conferences
Lynne:

We still go and help at the MÂCHÉ conference.

John:

Yes, we go and help out any way we can. One thing we enjoy is visiting with exhibitors. There are a number of exhibitors we really look forward to seeing each year.

Lynne:

The Heppners, from way up north, have been involved with MÂCHÉ as exhibitors for many years. They have done well with homeschooling a large family.

John:

They are a lot of fun. We've had many of them stay with us, and one thing we've really noticed is your house is cleaner when they leave than when they arrived.

Lynne:

Exhibitors like coming to MÂCHÉ.

John:

There are a number of them that say, "We really appreciate the personal touch," the youth bringing water around, just people taking a personal interest in them.

Another change in focus is, before, it was more people giving of themselves, but now, I think there is a tendency toward people saying, "What can I go to get?" Even going to the displays and spending time with the exhibitors and then going and buying stuff online because it's a couple of dollars cheaper—that grieves me. It's getting away from the personal, rather than saying, "We need to support these people." God is not poor.

I can remember people saying that MÂCHÉ conferences needed to be professional. We are to do things well, but we are not to emulate the world. We need to set aside that professional stereotype. People want to know we're real. People want to know the personal aspect.

I remember we would go to a lot of meetings all over the state. Sometimes it was tiring, but it was just tremendous to personally meet people and visit with them. Again, developing those personal relationships is encouraging. It really gets down to maintaining those personal relationships with each other.

Chapter Thirteen

The von Gohrens start home educating in the late seventies before it is legal and join the legislative battle for the freedom to homeschool in Minnesota. They become involved with MÂCHÉ and help coordinate a united effort to protect and defend homeschool freedoms. Pam is appointed to the Minnesota Nonpublic Education Council, where she continues to be active, promoting homeschooling.

Written Contribution Submitted (January 11, 2014) by: Pam von Gohren (Past MÂCHÉ Board Member and Past MÂCHÉ Legislative Liaison)
> Husband: *Jerry von Gohren (Past MÂCHÉ Board Member)*
> Children: *three sons, one daughter*

Pam:

A kaleidoscope of recollection tumbles in response to "What's a favorite home education memory?"

Our daughter being a member of the first (1986) MÂCHÉ graduation.

Our youngest son as student speaker for the 1996 Capitol rotunda rally celebrating 10,000 Home Educated Children in the Land of 10,000 Lakes.

We can't forget (then) U.S. Congressman Bill Frenzel's staff asking our family how they could assist home educators with special legislation or protection when our 1985 traveling U.S. history seminar (a.k.a. family vacation) brought us to Washington, D.C. "You are the first home educating family we've met; the children are so poised and articulate, even the two little guys!"

In 1983, our field trip to Pike Island Nature Center, where a confused, nervous staff thought the Minnetonka Home Education group was from the Hennepin County Home School (a residential facility for male juvenile delinquents), also located in Minnetonka. They were quite relieved to be working with well-behaved, eager-to-learn children!

The September morning we went shopping for cross-country ski boots at a large sport shop's annual sale, where the salesman, muttering, "Truants," and scoffing at the name of their school, challenged the boys' not being in class. "Guess you didn't see WCCO-TV news last night," the boys replied. "Hunter Academy [a.k.a. von Gohren homeschool] was the feature story."

Our four children say their favorite memory is of "superintendent drill." This drill was necessary because, in those days before home education was clearly legal, our district's assistant superintendent had vowed to ferret out every home educating family for prosecution. The same individual also chaired a blue-ribbon committee, of which Jerry was a key member, and they exchanged documents several times a week. A peculiar whine in the official's car's engine gave us a one-block-away alert signal, just enough time for the kids to move from sunny, dining room study hall to lower-level family room, out of a visitor's sight. Such breathless excitement they enjoyed, yet it was accompanied by sober thanksgiving that we were never discovered in the ten years we taught the children before the Definition of School bill [Compulsory Attendance bill H.F. 432] was passed in 1987.

The birth of Minnetonka Home Education Association in 1982 fulfilled a need for additional children to accompany ours on field trips to institutions that required minimum numbers for presentations. Convincing the Science Museum of Minnesota that a "group of elementary students" was equivalent to a class from an ungraded or open-style public school took many phone conversations. However, after the first visit was a rousing success, future reservations were welcomed. Word got around, and other venues followed suit.

The Law of 1987
Pam:

We saw God's Hand in so many instances through the years. When the Definition of School bill [Compulsory Attendance bill H.F. 432] was being debated (1985-1987), almost no reassuring statistics were available to convince legislators that home education was effective. However, Jerry's brother, a lobbyist in Washington State, prevailed upon the superintendent of public instruction for an embargoed report her office had compiled for the Washington legislature: a two-year-long study of home schooled children, which included their excellent nationally norm-referenced test scores. Express mailed, it arrived just in time for me to present at a key Senate hearing to the consternation of opponents who thought they had the Minnesota legislation beaten.

Creation of the Minnesota Nonpublic Education Council to advise the commissioner of education on private school matters was another provision in the Definition of School bill [Compulsory Attendance bill H.F. 432]. First appointed by Governor Ventura, I have been reappointed to the council by two subsequent administrations, all of different parties, prompting a council colleague to quip, "She 'plays well with others' despite strong convictions!"

The council gives opportunities to partner with other nonpublic school organizations—very helpful when there is a need to defend our collective rights, and it oversees accrediting organizations who provide accountability for families and schools who choose outside verification of their educational efforts. Meanwhile, Jerry's contribution to MÂCHÉ was the creation of the first website, developing electronic communication systems and generating many, many email alerts.

Other Significant Legislation
Pam:

Another instance occurred when a bill extending the compulsory attendance age to five-year-olds afforded me, as the MÂCHÉ legislative liaison, and Karl Bunday, of Minnesota Homeschooler's Alliance, opportunity to collaborate in defeating the proposal (1994-1995) with the encouragement of Senator Gen Olson, a key supporter who has become a special friend. We are all people of prayer; inspiration for acceptable compromise wording could only be attributed to Him who is Wisdom.

Prayer-walking the Capitol's halls was a daily discipline, as defending already won rights, and expanding opportunities for our students became the legislative focus in the 1990s.

Examples include: Take Credit for Learning—the education tax credit (1996-1997); inclusion of home educated students in the Post-Secondary Enrollment Option (1997); participation in high school athletics and extracurricular programs (1999); and parent-taught driver education (1999).

Recognizing the disastrous implications of Goals 2000/School-to-Work/Profile of Learning on the population as a whole plus potential intrusion into home education, our families put in much effort to defeat these programs in 1999-2000. Unfortunately, their principle objectives have returned in 2014 as Common Core and World's Best Workforce bills. Defending our freedom will always be necessary.

2001 Senate Hearing

Pam:

Families of all styles of home education protested in huge numbers against a 2001 bill requiring parents to hold a high school diploma before teaching their children. Overwhelmed by calls, Capitol phone lines shut down. Hearing room seating overflowed. Capitol hallways were clogged with families sitting calmly on the hard floors. Personnel from facility management, remembering our appreciative comments on legislative days, wheeled out television sets so folks could watch a closed-circuit broadcast of the hearing.

I coordinated the people who were to testify before the committee and the influx of supporters from out of state while caring for my seriously ill mother. Flying home while the hearing actually occurred was a three-hour prayer vigil. The Lord was generous. Disembarking my flight in Minneapolis, I found at my gate Chris Klicka, HSLDA attorney, who had testified at the hearing, waiting to board his flight home. We were able to have a quick debrief in the gate area along with exclamations of "Glory!"

The episode [the 2001 event] made such an impression on legislators from both sides of the aisle that it's been referenced often, even as recently as 2011, by an ideologically opposed member on an education committee, when the Reporting Mandate Reduction bill was in discussion. "You do not want to rile the homeschool community," the legislator warned newer committee members.

Respectful voices make lasting impressions!

Advice

Pam:

Our advice to present and future home educating parents is to *pray* continuously! The Lord equips those He calls, but we have to humbly listen and obey. He may send you down a unique path you will only understand years from now. How sad to miss the adventure by following too closely what others are doing, even other home educators.

Resist the tyranny of anxiously seeking the *best* curriculum; listen to your children's cues for what *fits* their style and interests.

Model becoming educated by seizing opportunities to develop skills and acquire knowledge yourself.

Keep before you the truth that children are the means that God uses for completing the growing-up process in adults. James 1:2-4 says, "Consider it a sheer gift, friends, when tests and challenges come to you from all sides. You know that under pressure, your faith-life is forced out into the open and shows its true colors. So don't try to get out of anything prematurely. Let it do its work so you become mature and well-developed, not deficient in any way." (The Message)

Chapter Fourteen

The Heppners attend one of the Moores' seminars and are convinced they should continue to homeschool despite it not yet being legal. Helping the Duersts with their Home Grown Kids booth, the Heppners attend MÂCHÉ for the first time. After several years they start Heppner and Heppner Construction and buy the Duerst's inventory. Vending and speaking for a number of years, they eventually sell their business to the Bjorkmans, who rename the business Heppner's Legacy Homeschool Resources.

Interview (November 26, 2013) with:
DuWayne "Spud" and **Miriam Heppner** (Heppner and Heppner Construction)
> Children: *Jemima, Benjamin, Samuel, Josiah, Joseph, Abraham, Micah, Moses, Solomon, Joanna, Susanna, Abigael, Elizabeth, Zachariah, Rebecca, Rachael, Avianna.*

Miriam:

I didn't go to kindergarten. My nine-year-old sister taught me to read when I was four, so I figured I could teach our oldest daughter, Jemima, how to read. I held Jemima back from kindergarten and bought a little phonics kit. I didn't see the necessity of kindergarten and didn't want to send her, mainly for socialization reasons.

I had heard from moms what happened when their kids went to school. They'd come home from school, and now "Mom doesn't know anything," and this wall happened between mother and child. Jemima and I had a close relationship, and I didn't want that to change.

DuWayne:

Miriam taught Jemima how to read. So we were basically homeschooling, but we didn't even know it. The principal came out and did a home visit with Jemima; he was flabbergasted at what she knew after just one year.

He was concerned about socialization, but as soon as he asked that question, the boys started coming downstairs. After the third boy came down, he said, "You probably don't have problems with socialization."

The Moores in Bemidji

Miriam:

We didn't know about MÂCHÉ at that time, but when Jemima was still five, Dan and Kathy Duerst invited Raymond and Dorothy Moore to speak in Bemidji [on July 15, 1984]. We went and heard them. That was pretty cool. It was a good-sized group. I was surprised. There were skeptical people there too.

DuWayne:

The Moores' seminar turned us in the direction of home-schooling, which I was interested in because I sensed Miriam's heart in wanting to connect with the kids.

Miriam:

We also got to meet and dialogue with the Moores in the Duerst's home after the seminar, which was really special.

DuWayne:

I remember asking Raymond Moore, "What kind of sacrifice does it take to homeschool?" At the time, I was kind of offended by his response, because he laughed and said, "It's not a sacrifice. It's doing the right thing." But he was right. It is the right choice. The Moores' seminar and other seminars convinced us we needed to be active in teaching our children.

I remember making the decision to homeschool, thinking, *Okay, if we are going to do this, I need to be prepared to go to jail for this.* There was no law at that time, and the new law could have gone either way. Homeschooling was a commitment, and in a way, that is what is lacking now. People have the view that this is the way it has always been, and nothing is going to change. But we are on the edge of losing our freedom to homeschool every time the legislature is in session.

Meeting John Eidsmoe
DuWayne:

We had the privilege of meeting John Eidsmoe, the attorney that helped us obtain the law we now have in Minnesota. We went to a seminar he did at Oak Hills Christian College in Bemidji and had lunch with him afterward.

Miriam:

He was traveling around different places in the state to get a grassroots feel of "What should this law look like?" We learned so much in that seminar, like this law needed to not only be everything we want, but also something the legislature would look at and say, "Yes, this is good." That was a huge learning experience for us, and just being with like-minded people really helped to solidify what we were doing.

The previous law had been declared unconstitutionally vague, but homeschooling still wasn't something people were broadcasting.

We were the first homeschoolers that we know of in our school district. Because of our excitement over homeschooling, others became interested and asked questions like "Why aren't you sending Jemima to school?" and "What do you use for curriculum?"

We started having parties in our home. We'd have food, and they could come in and see what we had. It gave us a chance to share what we were doing. A number of families started homeschooling because of that.

Originally, we were helping Dan and Kathy Duerst with their business, the Riverside Schoolhouse Resource Center, named because they'd bought an old schoolhouse outside of Bemidji for their store. They were on the cutting edge of the eclectic Christian curriculum business, and it grew to be quite big. They traveled all over the United States.

DuWayne:

I think the enemy knew that, and that's why they struggled. It was the same with us, and I told Brad and Nancy Bjorkman too, "This business/ministry is not liked by the enemy. He is going to hit your marriage more than anything, just like he has us and the previous family." It's not the homeschooling the enemy is mad about; it's the salvation of souls.

<u>Going to MÂCHÉ with the Duersts</u>

Miriam:

The first time we went to MÂCHÉ was to help Dan and Kathy at their booth, which was known as "The Home Grown Kids booth."

That first year attending MÂCHÉ, I had in my mind what homeschoolers were like. You know, they were the people with long braided hair and the long jean skirt and boots, and I was surprised because there were people in their sports getup, like they had just come in from running. There were those in their high heels and makeup, very professional looking and talking with an extensive vocabulary. Then there were people like us, and then the normal ones. Every kind of person was there, and it was like "Wow! Homeschooling is not just for weirdos like us." It was pretty cool.

<u>Heppner and Heppner Construction</u>

Miriam:

In 1985, we established Heppner and Heppner Construction as a book business and started as Home Grown Kids distributors.

DuWayne:

We really started our business to get materials cheaper for ourselves.

Miriam:

Wholesale. We had so many kids (I was expecting our fifth).

DuWayne:

That is how Dan and Kathy approached us. "With your number of children, you are going to need these materials. If you sign on as distributors, you can sell them and get them at a reduced price for yourselves."

Miriam:

It also helped them in their effort, because then we were under them.

DuWayne:

I had a construction company, and now with this Home Grown Kids line, we needed a tax ID and name. The construction and homeschooling resources played off each other. "Heppner and Heppner Construction. Building homes and families. Providing you with the tools you need." It was a name people remembered.

Heppner and Heppner Construction at MÂCHÉ

DuWayne:

In 1990, Dan and Kathy pulled back and weren't doing their business anymore, and so the next year they did not go to MÂCHÉ. Miriam and I went for the first time, just as attendees, and walked through the vendor hall.

Miriam:

We could hear people asking, "Do you know where the Home Grown Kids booth is?" They were looking for a booth where they could customize their children's education.

In the beginning, you couldn't get the majority of even the boxed curriculum created for Christian schools, because homeschooling was not credible yet. The big curriculum sellers didn't want to have legal issues. Eventually there were a few who said, "Yes, homeschooling is viable now," but there were still very few booths. So we saw a huge need.

DuWayne:

That is what gave us the vision to bring back the "Home Grown Kids" booth.

In 1992, we went back as vendors to MÂCHÉ, and I remember standing in the middle of our booth unable to move. People were handing me money and taking things off the shelf. I had no clue what they were buying. It was a feeding frenzy. Parents had finally found something they could use to homeschool their kids.

Miriam:

Before there were a lot of other vendors, we would get calls from people who just wanted one of our catalogs. They couldn't even get close enough to our booth to get a catalog. That is how crazy it was.

DuWayne:

When other vendors came in, I was worried. "How are we going to make it?" But we couldn't meet all of the needs there.

Miriam:

In doing research and looking for items I needed for our kids, I'd share what I'd found, and if I thought it was in the excellent category, I'd add it to our catalog. We went from half of an eight-by-eleven sheet to a twenty-eight-page catalog and an extensive website.

MÂCHÉ conferences are some of our kids' favorite memories. It was a business, run by our family. It was fun to put the kids into jobs that went along with their gifts, and we enjoyed working together.

Many years we would say, "This is getting to be too much." I remember fasting and praying and, as a family, asking, "What do You have for us here, God?" Each time God would show us in miraculous ways that He was still in the business. I remember DuWayne saying, "Now, until God says, 'You're done,' it's not 'Why are we doing this?' but 'How can we do this differently?'"

We streamlined processes, like building the displays the Bjorkmans are still using, so we could have most of our books set up in the shelves before we left our storefront, rather than the books all being in boxes.

<u>Workshops</u>

Miriam:

The workshops we gave came about because of hard times, what was working to fill a need, and what God was teaching us. Whatever God allowed us to go through as a family, in our marriage, or in homeschooling, we learned and shared with others.

Miriam and DuWayne Heppner with their daughter Susanna

Vending at MÂCHÉ

DuWayne:

Working with MÂCHÉ through the years, we've found them to be a model organization. And most of the vendors we've talked with have said, "MÂCHÉ is the best."

Miriam:

And these vendors have traveled all over the U.S.

DuWayne:

I think the biggest thing about MÂCHÉ is their servant heart. They aren't saying, "Follow us. We're going in the right direction." Instead, they bring people along. "This is the wagon we're pulling. Jump in if you want to come."

We got to know different board members like the Cookes, Biedermans, Lindstroms, and Schurkes and have been blessed to visit and stay in most of their homes. They weren't just homeschool people. They helped in any area they could, and it shows in the way the MÂCHÉ organization has been run and has kept running.

Miriam:

I don't know what I would have done through the years without Ruth Lindstrom and Lynne Cooke. They are two very dear older sisters in Christ . . . so encouraging.

Homeschool Family Camp

DuWayne:

Cookes used to participate in homeschool family camp up in Lake Bronson. Those camps were a lot of fun. We had a lot of Canadians come down for that too.

Miriam:

That was awesome, and it was very well attended.

DuWayne:

We got to encourage one another and have fun too. Campfires were always good; people would gather around. The Waldorfs were instrumental in organizing that.

Miriam:

We enjoyed getting together with the other vendors after MÂCHÉ. We didn't see each other usually more than once or twice a year, but we got so close. We would pray for each other through the year.

DuWayne:

The vendors at MÂCHÉ became family. You start out in business thinking, *There's my competition.* But you realize other vendors have the same struggles.

One year our bus broke down in Duluth on the loading dock while everyone else was waiting. I couldn't get it moved because it was a fuel issue. We had to tow it. A two dollar wire cost six hundred dollars to fix. The vendors were trying to help. I remember Barry Stebbing praying with me, and people giving us money to help.

The vendors were like family, just like the MÂCHÉ people.

Miriam:

It was kind of cool, how we helped each other. Like with Lifetime Books, we would say, "You know we are totally out of stock on that." or "We don't carry that, but I bet Lifetime does."

And they would do the same for us or other businesses. We helped each other unload and load, too.

People would say, "You must be so exhausted after MÂCHÉ." And I was exhausted, and yet there was this life in me. It wasn't physical. When you go to MÂCHÉ, the Holy Spirit is there in a big way. It is very edifying.

MÂCHÉ is not primarily about curriculum; it's about people sharing God. Even when I was giving and ministering, I was receiving and learning so much more. There is nothing I could have done that would have fed me as much as that.

Selling the Bjorkmans the Business
Miriam:

In 2006, we sold the business to the Bjorkmans. We brought the whole store down and left it with them, and that same trip, we finalized our adoption with our Avianna and brought her home. It was the best trade ever!

The first year we came and helped the Bjorkmans, I was standing back watching Brad and Nancy at work, and I thought, *They are doing such a great job. They are God's people for this.* But I was also really struggling with "Why didn't I step back earlier?"

I carry with me a lot of regret because this ministry/business took so much of my time and energy away from my family, especially my older kids. I know my kids have good memories of helping with MÂCHÉ and other conferences, but what bothers me is that the older kids grew up with us being so busy.

God knew what was going on in my heart though, and He had people come, one after another, throughout that whole convention. "This is what you said in your workshop." "You said this to me at your booth." "You prayed with me about this." There were all these testimonies. It was like God had scheduled them throughout the whole weekend. It was absolutely amazing. It was God's grace.

That year I moved from total regret to "Yes, God was in this and has used it." Hearing stories like "I was a mom with all of these responsibilities, and I thought, *If Miriam can do it with that number of kids, I can do it.* I went to your organization talk, and I thought, *I can go home and start putting this stuff to use.* And now look, this is our last kid and they're graduating." and "Our marriage would not have made it, if it wasn't for you guys sharing with us." This woman's story was God saying, "I was in this. Even though things got off balance, I used this." He encouraged my heart.

Favorite Memories

Miriam:

I remember the first time I really grasped the idea of delight-directed studies. It was spring, and our little Sam couldn't concentrate on school. He just wanted to get outside. He was looking outside, and all these butterflies were flying around. He asked, "Where were they in the winter, Mom?" I said, "Let's do some research and find out."

We didn't have internet back then, so we pulled out the books we had on butterflies. We incorporated science, history, geography, and art. We had so much fun, and the kids remember that to this day. That helped me break out as a mom and enjoy the learning process rather than just schooling.

DuWayne:

That's some of my memories too, coming home and Miriam and the kids showing me things that they'd learned, the kids helping one another with math or different projects, or showing each other easier ways to do things. It's just fun to see that in the home, the delight and joy they have in learning. The struggles too helped them learn how to persevere.

Miriam:

Another favorite memory: Solomon, who was probably three at the time, would sit and play Legos while we worked on memorizing the first three chapters of Genesis. I figured he was in his own little world, not taking in anything.

Well, a couple years later, it was that record cold winter. I hadn't stepped foot outside for two weeks, and DuWayne had been gone on a commercial job. I was going crazy, totally.

The kids assigned to make lunch were not getting lunch done, and I was like, "Just get the meal on the table!" So we finally got the meal on the table, and someone was *click, clink, clinking*, with their silverware.

I had been training myself not to yell, so the words came out very staccato. "Don't touch your silverware until we are ready to eat." We served the meal and sat down, and someone was picking at their food before the prayer. "And don't touch your food until we pray!" Everyone's like, "Okay, Mom."

Well, little Solomon pipes up, "And the Lord God said, 'Thou shalt not eat of the food in the midst of your plate, neither shall you touch it, lest you die!'" Two years later, he remembered the verse and paraphrased it. That was pretty cool.

DuWayne:

That shows they pick up on a lot even without us being aware of it.

Miriam:

Our Solomon is now in the U.S. Air Force. I am thankful I have taken time for Scripture memory with our kids.

Advice

DuWayne:

Like Raymond Moore said, "It's not a sacrifice at all. It's doing the right thing." Know that you need to be committed. It's not just "I'll try this because it's a fad" or "It's working for them." Make sure God is leading you. Listen to His direction, and be obedient.

Miriam:

My question to the next generation is "What legacy are you leaving?" We're at a stage in life now where we see it's not just about our kids; it's also about our grandkids. The atmosphere we raise our kids in is usually going to be what our grandkids are raised in. It's not just about the here and now. It's about each moment being an opportunity to know Christ more and to build our relationships with Him.

DuWayne:

The most important things are relationships—relationships we and our children have with Christ, the relationships we have with our children, and the relationship we have as husband and wife. That's what homeschooling is really about. It's not just about making good children but godly children.

Miriam:

As moms struggling with patience, we need to work at creating a home atmosphere of joy and at crying out to Jesus regularly on behalf of ourselves and our children. As we cry out to Jesus, He really does work in us. He comes in and becomes the great I AM in our lives. I wish I had grasped hold of that earlier. I was more about surviving and getting through the moment. Now I'm seeing that the journey is really what's important, because our relationship with Christ is the destination.

Miriam:

Where are those areas where we are not being Christ-like? Needing and exemplifying Christ more and more is the legacy I would like to leave for the next generation and generations.

Chapter Fifteen

The McMillins become Christians and begin homeschooling just as it becomes legal. They connect with Ruth and Dean Lindstrom and, through them, MÂCHÉ. When one of their children faces a set of learning challenges, a MÂCHÉ vendor is able to help. The McMillins continue to persevere, homeschooling for over twenty-five years.

Interview (August 8, 2013) with:
Jerry and **Linda McMillin** (Homeschool Pioneers)
      Children: *Kelly, Corrie, Luke, Josiah, Hannah, Abigail*

Linda:

We started homeschooling in 1987. It was just legal. We actually became Christians about the time our oldest son was born.

We were really developing a whole new philosophy on education. We wanted a Christian education for our children. When Focus on the Family had that fifteen-minute radio broadcast with Dr. Raymond Moore, I thought, *This is it.*

Jerry:

Once I heard that program, I thought, *That's crazy, but that's right.* I never really hesitated from there on. Working a 1:00 p.m. to 9:00 p.m. shift, I probably wouldn't have seen my kids if they were in a traditional school setting.

Linda:

I ordered Dr. Raymond Moore's books and read them all. They were really the only books out there on homeschooling.

Jerry:

His books were definitely very influential.

Linda:

Teaching Home magazine [founded in 1980] was also a big encouragement, because it gave us connection, even though our kids did joke about the "perfect family" pictures, where they'd all dress alike.

Jerry:

We went to the kindergarten roundup, I think for documentation-type purposes. It was in our local public school library. On display, in a prominent position as we walked in the door, was a book about evolution being true. I thought, *That is why we're not coming here.* If I needed any confirmation perhaps that was it.

Linda:

The interesting thing was the attitude toward homeschooling back then. People didn't know what homeschooling was, and they were really negative.

Jerry:

The church had kind of a "wait and see what happens" take.

Linda:

We talked to Ruth and Dean Lindstrom from Rochester, and they encouraged us. Ruth talked me into making a theme and a mission statement and a name and all that. You needed an identity, especially back then, when writing to the public school.

Our town is known for its eagles, so I had a friend draw up a design. I also found all of the kids these jackets at the flea market with the logo "Green Valley Christian School," so we named our homeschool Green Valley Christian School.

When we were first starting, I visited with another family in the area. The mom was frustrated. Her son was in kindergarten, and I said, "You've really got to listen to Dr. Dobson." She was hesitant at first, but I was thinking, *I don't want to do this homeschool thing alone.* They did decide to pull their son out, and they started homeschooling the year after we did.

Our kids always felt like they were missing riding the school bus. So a tradition for us was I would put the kids in the little red wagon and pull them up and down the street at the beginning of every year.

McMillin's Homeschool School Bus.
Standing: Kelly *Riding*: Luke and Corrie

When they finally did ride a school bus, they said, "This is really icky." I said, "I told you. I rode a lot of school buses, and it's not really what it is cracked up to be."

First Day Homeschooling
Linda:

I remember our first day of homeschooling. Our son's assignment was to draw our house. He never liked to color or anything like that.

Well, you'd have thought I'd asked him to build a house. I was really hesitant at that point. I can remember thinking, *How am I ever going to do this?* But I guess we made it. That son is now a police officer. The Lord used the skills he does have.

At one point, he had a job at the jail. I find this kind of hilarious; he said, "You know, Mom, I never really learned how to talk like those high school students. I've a bit of a hard time with their vocabulary." That and better penmanship were the only things he ever commented on as lacking in his education.

I don't think either was too much of a lack. He homeschools his children today; that's a blessing. His wife wasn't homeschooled, so it's a big jump for her. It's kind of funny. She was more gung ho about homeschooling than he was. Because Jerry participated so much, I think our son was nervous about his part.

Jerry:

I taught language and physical education. We would go ice skating and shovel in between sessions. I remember spending hours learning how to teach reading. Now I look back and think that seems ridiculous, but we had to start somewhere. There's pressure to get it done and do it right, and reading is one thing that's pretty critical.

Linda:

We always felt like people were testing our children when we took them out places, especially in those early years. People would give them a book just to see how well they could read.

I did the sciences and the math, and when we got to chemistry, I remember sitting outside with the chemistry book, trying to learn it. We only had the answers, no solutions. When I couldn't figure it out, I'd go to our son. He never tested very well in chemistry, but he was really good at helping me figure it out.

Our two oldest did a lot of their subjects together, even though they were three years apart. Our daughter would get A's on the test and not understand it at all, and our son would struggle with it and maybe get a C. I always said, "He really deserved the A's he earned."

On school days, we didn't take our kids downtown during the day, and we were really cautious about them being outside even in the yard. You thought you needed to let your neighbors know what you were doing, so that they didn't report you. But it was never a problem for us—I think because we had built relationships with them.

We shoveled most of our neighbors' driveways for them. I think once we did fifteen driveways. Anybody elderly, we shoveled their snow, it seemed. It was the way we brought up our kids—look out for the elderly and help them.

One of our neighbors was a retired school teacher. When we moved in, she showed up on our doorstep with cookies, and she and her husband became like our kids' grandparents. They were both wonderful. My kids were over there more often than the couple's own grandkids.

They both ended up getting Alzheimer's. Her family took her someplace, but the husband stayed. He couldn't spend nights by himself. So our oldest son spent three or four nights a week with him. Sometimes I think that's where he decided he wanted to be a cop, because they would watch Andy Griffith.

Concern from Family

Linda:

We really didn't get any comments from family. We had a sister-in-law who was a public school teacher. Jerry's mom would never comment on anything. The only thing I ever heard from my mom was—and becoming Christians and everything at the same time, we probably seemed a little fanatical—she said, "I figured you would do something like that."

Later on when our son had extra educational needs, she was very concerned about homeschooling. I think she was pretty pleased, though, to see how it turned out for him.

Our family has also been blown away by our kids' vocabulary, especially the younger kids, because having older kids around, the younger kids pick up such an excellent vocabulary.

MÂCHÉ Conferences

Linda:

We heard about the MÂCHÉ conferences through Ruth and Dean, and going was really a big encouragement. I remember Roger Schurke with these different hats. He always had a good sense of humor. We have only missed maybe two MÂCHÉ conferences. I remember some of the first curriculum sellers we saw at MÂCHÉ's early conferences. It was just in this little gym. There was A Beka, Bob Jones, and Weaver.

At MÂCHÉ one year, they were giving away a CD to whoever had been homeschooling the longest. I thought, *I have a chance at this one. I've been doing this for twenty-two years.* Somebody beat me by two years.

We are MÂCHÉ members and HSLDA [Home School Legal Defense Association] members. I should have bought a life-long membership to HSLDA. We have well surpassed it. But we feel we need to keep supporting HSLDA, because it's a good thing. Mike Farris and Chris Klicka from HSLDA came to Minnesota a lot in those early days.

Interacting with the School District
Linda:

We had some struggles with our school district over testing and reporting. Starting in first grade, they insisted my son come into the public school to do the standardized testing. I had little ones, so my husband went—our insistence was our son was not going in there unless we came with him.

They put our son in the first-grade classroom with all of the other kids, and I remember my son saying, "All they do is get up and sharpen their pencils. It's very distracting." The other kids were so busy looking at him I don't think they did very well.

The next day they put Jerry and our son in a room with just a teacher's aide to give the test. The aide tried to talk Jerry into putting our son back into school.

We did the testing that way the first year, then said, "We're not doing this again." We asked our neighbor and told the public school, "We are going to have this retired teacher give the test." She supervised our testing for a number of years and had no qualms about us homeschooling.

At first, we could only get the tests from the school, and they made it such a hassle. HSLDA wrote our superintendent a couple of times.

Jerry:

Our superintendent wasn't real friendly toward home education. That was pretty intimidating to go through, but I was glad HSLDA was there to call.

Linda:

In 1993, we had to get the superintendent's signature to get the tests, but he returned our request to us unsigned. Then we had to deal with a counselor to get them. And then, just so someone could verify that we did not cheat, we had to have someone there, and they wanted results, a score or grade equivalent.

In 1994, they would not give us the tests to take home. We thought, *Good! Then you won't get the results.* We finally figured out how to get our own tests through Christian Liberty, and we switched the time we gave the tests and told the school district, "Oh, well, we're already all done."

I've gotten to know the superintendent's wife. Once she brought up socialization and teaching chemistry. I said, "I just learned the chemistry along with my kids. And I had a friend; she wasn't highly educated, worked full-time, single mom, had three kids, and homeschooled. Her kids pretty much had to do a lot on their own. Her daughter is a chemist at a big university today. So, I don't think that's an issue."

Homeschooling in the Hospital

Linda:

Our son Luke was born the year we started homeschooling in 1987. A month after he was born, he had to go back into the hospital for a week. So we actually did our homeschooling in the hospital. You kind of become ambassadors for homeschooling.

Luke had a lot of ear infections and things as a child, and he was also burned over a good percentage of his body. He pulled a pan off his grandmother's stove, which had hamburger and water in it. It was pretty major. Normally they would have sent him to the burn unit, but they kept him here because the doctor here had worked in a burn center. Our son was in the hospital recovering from that, so again, we did school in the hospital.

They say some of those injuries, between the head and ears, can cause some delays. Luke had speech issues. He jabbered a mile a minute, but we couldn't really understand him. We had him tested, and he had issues with his hearing. We also tested him for speech. We went into the special education department and started him with a speech therapist.

Minnesota Vision Center
Linda:

When Luke was thirteen, the Minnesota Learning Enhancement Center was handing out information from the Minnesota Vision Center at the MÂCHÉ conference. They had a checklist, and I said, "Well, we could check almost everything on this list." We went to that workshop, and I thought, *This fits Luke to a T.*

So we had him tested in Minneapolis at the Vision Center. One of the women there said, "It's remarkable he can read this well for the vision issues he has."

During the testing, they put him on this computer, and you could see where his eyes went on the page. He had major tracking and focusing problems with his eyes. Yet, he had twenty-twenty vision.

When we took him to the local eye doctor for an eye test, the doctor scolded him up and down for being lazy about reading. I stopped the doctor and said, "No, that is not the issue."

We did Luke's actual vision therapy in La Crosse, and they said, "It is so nice he was homeschooled. He doesn't even know he has a problem." We actually had to convince him that he needed to do therapy. We did an hour of therapy every day for a long time.

They had a reading specialist; we had him work with him. Also, a friend of ours worked at the dyslexic center over in Rochester, and she worked with him too. Of course, he never wanted to be diagnosed as dyslexic, but the gal that worked with him said he is both auditory and visually dyslexic, and he has a processing issue.

When he was in tenth grade, I would have said, "No way will this child go to college." He got to college, and I told them, "He's probably going to need help. He's probably not going to ask for it," etc.

They put him on probation. He was not very happy with me. After the first semester, the school wanted to know why I thought he needed to be on probation. He was a straight A student. Blew me away. He was a straight A student all the way through college.

Jerry:

The kids learned what they needed to learn. Obviously every kid is different. Our oldest daughter we didn't have to teach to read. She is one of those kids that at age five took off. Then our middle son comes along, and he really can't read until he's twelve because of his vision issues.

MÂCHÉ Vendors

Linda:

The MÂCHÉ conferences have always been so good for finding what you need.

Jerry:

Something that really made a difference was the phonics program that we used for all six kids. It's called Professor Phonics.

Linda:

Our grandchildren are using it too. It was one of only a few phonics-based programs there.

Jerry:

With MÂCHÉ specifically, we've appreciated the expertise of the vendors from day one. Over the years, I think we have used the expertise of the vendors in probably every subject.

Linda:

Because we have gone for so many years, it's like seeing old friends.

Connecting Generations

Linda:

A couple of years ago Ruth Lindstrom gave a talk about connecting generations, and I thought, *Has the Lord placed me here to be a connection between one generation and the next?*

Over the years things have changed so much. When we first started homeschooling, supporting one another—moms getting together, talking, and sharing curriculum and ideas—was really important. But with the advent of the internet and information being so readily available, I don't think people feel that need. But I think they still do need that people connection.

I've struggled with how to encourage people to keep making that connection. The best way, I've found, is through field trips.

Jerry:

"Let us run with endurance the race set before us, fixing our eyes on Jesus Christ, the author and perfecter of our faith" (Hebrews 12:1-2). You can't possibly do it on your own. I was just adding it up this morning, so far sixty-five school years of education—that is a lot of spelling!

Advice

Jerry:

A homeschool speaker at MÂCHÉ two years ago said, "We teach what we know. We reproduce what we are."

One of my favorite verses is Isaiah 40:31: "Those who hope in the Lord shall renew their strength. They shall soar on wings like eagles. They will not grow weary. They will walk and not faint." Stay focused on the Lord is my best advice.

Chapter Sixteen

Maren Stowman is a homeschooler whose father has the love and conviction to move his family away from the public school to a place where they can do what God has called them to do.

Written Contribution Submitted (November 20, 2013) by: Maren Stowman (Homeschool Graduate)

Maren:

We lived in the neat, old house where my dad had grown up. At one time the front room had housed the local telephone switchboard where an operator sat connecting customers' calls.

One noon when Dad walked home for lunch, he found me on my bicycle out on the front sidewalk. Instead of riding back and forth, I was sitting, staring at the children playing on the school playground. My neighborhood friends and the kids I knew from church were out on their noon recess.

My dad walked into the house and announced to my mom that we were moving. He had no idea where we were going, but he knew he had to move his daughters away from the school if our homeschool was to survive.

Thus began the months of searching the countryside for a home and also of studying house plans with the possibility of building. By God's providence, a friend realized what we were up to when he returned our books of house plans to the library for us. The night before my youngest sister was born, my parents made the decision to accept the offer our friend had given us to move into a house he owned three miles out of town.

Two months later in cold February, friends and family formed a giant team and moved us into our new home—a home so well suited for us with no painting or remodeling required.

To this day I wonder at the convictions and selfless love that led my parents to turn their backs on all that was familiar. It was the first move of my dad's life, and it meant leaving behind the place where my parents had made their first home together. It was a house full of memories, and yet the past was not as important to them as their daughters' future.

I grew up hearing this story, and I'm convinced that partly because of it, I took what my parents were doing seriously. Homeschooling was serious to them. It had to do with their faith in Christ and with all of life. It has become that to me, as well.

Chapter Seventeen

As MÂCHÉ's legislative liaison, John Tuma works to help make Post-Secondary Enrollment Options more accessible to homeschool students. Homeschoolers are allowed access to public schools' extracurricular activities without having to pay extra, and homeschoolers defeat a Senate bill that proposed placing new requirements on homeschoolers.

Interview (December 1, 2012) with:

John Tuma (MÂCHÉ's Legislative Liaison and MÂCHÉ Board Member)

      Wife: *Wendy (MÂCHÉ Board Member)*

      Children: *Cal, Molly*

PSEO (Post-Secondary Enrollment Options)
John:

Before the PSEO law was amended in 1997, Minnesota homeschoolers essentially enrolled in the public school and then just signed up for all PSEO courses [duel high school and college credit].

It was a hassle, because the public school didn't know if the homeschool student really qualified. Now this student is enrolled in the public school for their last two years, so was the public school supposed to give them a diploma?

A lot of tension surrounded PSEO, and it created an opportunity for us. We said, "Hey, why not just have the students apply right to whatever school they want to take PSEO courses through? The colleges are the ones getting the money anyway, so make them do the work."

The public schools were like "That's a good deal. Then it's their problem." So in 1997, the legislature amended the PSEO law so that nonpublic school and homeschool students could participate in the program without having to enroll in their local public high schools.

Extracurricular Activities
John:

In 1999, the legislature changed the law to require the local public school to make available to resident homeschool students their extracurricular activities, and the legislature prohibited the public school from charging an extra fee for the right to participate.

That was kind of a funny thing, because the then-Speaker of the House Phil Carruthers had neighbors who were liberal friends of theirs who homeschooled, and their kids wanted to go to band at the local public school. The school district said, "Well, you can be in band, but you have to pay two thousand dollars because we want you to pay a proportional share of the teacher's salary."

Phil's like "What do you mean?" So he called up the superintendent and said, "What are you talking about?" The superintendent blew him off. Well, you don't blow off the Speaker of the House. You just don't.

Guess what, now we have a law that says, "You have to let homeschool students participate." We had it before Tim Tebow [the first homeschooled student to win the Heisman Trophy; Tim Tebow is known for promoting homeschoolers' access to public school extracurricular activities].

2001 Senate Hearing
John:

In 2001, Christine Jax came along. She was commissioner of education, and she's like "Why are these homeschoolers doing these tests, and we don't get to see the scores?"

She introduces a bill, and tucked away in her department bill, on the last couple of pages, was a revision forcing homeschoolers to give their test scores to the Department of Education. It was a big bill, and when that provision was loaded on, it became a big deal. Fortunately, the Republicans were in charge of the House at the time, but the Senate was still DFL [Democratic-Farmer-Labor].

On March 21, 2001, the Senate had a hearing, and it was a huge event for us homeschoolers. We flooded the Capitol. The place was just packed. The whole hallway, what we would call the east wing, had TVs to view what was happening.

When someone testifying at the hearing said something negative, you could hear booing muffled in the background, and when someone said something positive, the halls outside would erupt in cheers. But inside, the hearing room stayed quiet as could be. A lot of people testified that day, and they voted it down.

I later searched the *Senate Briefly,* which is the Senate's weekly magazine, and was really surprised. I couldn't find a thing. All they had was this cute picture at the hearing of little Erin Erpelding testifying. I think the DFL senators didn't want it to get out to the public in their publication that they had been foolish enough to take on the homeschoolers. So all we got was this nice picture of a homeschooling family, happy in front of the Senate.

Chapter Eighteen

Senator Gen Olson speaks to Senator Pappas about newly proposed homeschool requirements and warns her that the homeschoolers will respond with a strong lobbying effort.

Interview (January 22, 2013) with:
Senator Gen Olson (A Friend of Homeschoolers)

The 2001 Senate Hearing
Gen:

A proposal came out of the Department of Education [2001], putting requirements on reporting and requiring a high school diploma for teachers in homeschools. The chair of the committee it was going before, Senator Pappas, seemed to think these requirements perfectly reasonable. I got word the stops were ready to be pulled out, and an email message was going to go around the state telling homeschoolers to start calling in to the chair's office and others on the committee. I said to the person who was going to tell people to start calling in, "Before you do that, give me one more chance. I'll talk to Senator Pappas."

I went and found where she was in committee. I asked if she'd come out, and I said, "I just want to check what you plan to do with these provisions on homeschooling, because," I said, "there is going to be a strong lobbying effort. I just wanted to forewarn you, and I wanted to know if you are, in fact, intending to go forward with this." She said, "The requirements seem perfectly reasonable to me." So yes, she was planning on going forward. I said, "Okay."

So many people called in, it actually shut down the phone lines in the Capitol.

We came into the hearing room that day, and the sergeants had set up TVs out in the halls, because the seats were all filled and there were groups out in the hall. It was another situation where every child was perfectly quiet and well behaved.

There had been a very careful plan of selecting the people, not a whole lineup of people coming up to whine about this or that, but a very well-done presentation on these issues.

It came to the vote. There were, at least, two major issues, and somebody had asked that we vote on them separately. I called for roll call on both of them. You can't fudge that, and they went down in flames. I think there were only one or two brave souls who actually voted in favor. That, to me, was a highlight.

Chapter Nineteen

The Erpeldings start homeschooling when they realize they are barely seeing their children. They get involved legislatively, and Bonnie and her eight-year-old daughter both testify at a Senate hearing and help to defeat the bill proposing new regulations on homeschoolers. They join the board of the Dodge County Homeschooling Association and volunteer at MÂCHÉ conferences.

Interview (August 8, 2013) with:

Bonnie Erpelding (Board Member of the Dodge County Home School Association)

> Husband: *Rick (Board Member of the Dodge Country Home School Association)*
> Children: ***Erin**, Ryan, Kelly, Ricky, Abigail*

Bonnie:

When Erin, my oldest, was five, I really felt convicted. At that time, I had three beautiful children, but I didn't see them much because they were at daycare. I was working full-time in Rochester, and my husband worked in Owatonna, so he had a forty-five-minute commute.

Life was very harried. I was running in the morning, getting the kids breakfast, getting them off to daycare, picking them up, and then in the evening we fed them, bathed them, put them to bed, and we started over again in the morning. I suddenly realized I was not really the primary influence in their lives; neither of us was.

We started praying about it, and God put neighbors in our lives. One was just across the street, a very fun-loving lady who was very vocal about homeschooling. She would say, "Why don't you just homeschool them?" While we were living in Rochester, there was a homeschooler down this street and a homeschooler down that street. And we started thinking, *Why not?*

In April of 1998, we attended our first MÂCHÉ conference. We were thoroughly overwhelmed. But it struck us, if all of these thousands of people were considering doing this, surely we could do this.

A real heart tug came when I took Erin and Ryan to daycare, and Ryan started saying, "Why can't we just stay home like a family?" He was four years old, and he'd figured this thing out before his thirty-something-year-old mom did.

I used to go to work crying, thinking, *It just doesn't seem right to drop my kids off.* Even though they were with a wonderful Christian daycare mom, it just wasn't home. So I started homeschooling in the fall of 1998, really to spend time with my kids. That's what got me started.

We became very excited and encouraged when Erin jumped up out of the couch one day and said, "I can read!" I imagine it's like this with a lot of homeschool moms—you just don't really know what you can do. You don't know if it is going to work.

When Erin jumped out of the couch, I didn't even know she could read. We were just doing a homemade phonics program. I hadn't even bought a phonics book yet. I was just going through what I remembered, and actually thoroughly enjoying it.

My kids were five, four, and two at the time. We did all of those nice creative things you do those first couple of years, like making log cabins out of our sandwiches and building gingerbread houses. When I discovered it really came very simply for Erin to learn how to read, it really encouraged me.

It wasn't until we started having more community with other homeschoolers, attending more conferences, reading more books, spending more time teaching our kids about the Lord, and finding out how fun it was to be home with them that I got sold on it.

Concerns about Homeschooling
Bonnie:

To be honest, my first concern when starting was "Could we live on a single income?" I had a wonderful supervisor who said, "Take a year off. We will hold your job for you." That was a security net for me, but as we got to the end of the first year, it was so apparent that this was working and that this was what God wanted us to do. God was blessing it. Financially we were fine. To this day, it's just never been a problem.

Another potential concern was how to explain our decision to homeschool to extended family members and friends that disagreed. We have public school teachers among our family and friends. It wasn't so much that we wanted their approval, but we wanted to be able to live harmoniously with them. It wasn't really a problem, but nonetheless, we just had to psych ourselves up when spending holidays and vacations with them. What questions were we going to answer? How were we going to answer them? We had to have some savvy with how we did that.

Now that our older kids are graduated and are successful, socially and academically, both of our families have really, I think, embraced homeschooling and even support it.

Legislative Involvement
Bonnie:

Because we were planning on sending Erin to public school originally, we were very active following education policies at the local and at the state level. My husband and I got involved politically, trying to eliminate the "Profile of Learning." So the "Profile of Learning" handed down from "Goals 2000" is really what launched us into educational policy.

2001 Senate Hearing
Bonnie:

Getting involved in the 2001 State Senate Education Committee hearing was a complete accident. I had only been homeschooling for about three years. We were part of this little nondescript group locally. We weren't members of RAACHE (Rochester Area

Association of Christian Home Educators), nor were we involved in MÂCHÉ.

Well, the lady who was the president at that time of the Dodge County Homeschool Association called me up. She had slipped on the ice and broken her arm.

She was in such pain. She said, "Can you please go up and testify at this hearing?" I felt a little bit like "Well, I don't know if I am the best person." She said, "I know it would be better for you to go and do something rather than nothing at all."

At this hearing, there were two things going on. One had to do with standardized testing and whether or not we had to turn our tests into the school district. The other thing was whether or not you should be allowed to homeschool if you didn't have a high school diploma.

Two days before the hearing, I was on our computer, and Erin, who was eight at the time, wandered into the den. I asked her, "What would you say to someone if they told you you couldn't help homeschool because you didn't have a high school diploma?" I had to explain what a high school diploma was at that point.

She had already been helping me teach her seven-year-old and five-year-old siblings. I said, "Would you be willing to tell a group of people how important it is that you be able to continue to teach your brother and sister?"

She started talking, and I typed. We ended up with this one-page speech that, in summary, said, "It just seems like people shouldn't need to have a piece of paper to qualify them to tutor or mentor or teach another person."

In addition, we had a dear friend in Rochester, Buck Zobel, who had an incredible story. He's deceased now, but he'd lived through World War I and World War II. I knew he hadn't graduated from high school. He'd barely got through the ninth grade. When World War I started, he'd had to come home and work on the farm, but he was very successful in life at whatever he put his hand to. He did every profession you can think of. He and his wife raised four kids, and they were a well-knit family.

I called Buck, and I said, "Hey, Buck, you want to go to the Capitol with us?" He said, "You know I'm almost ninety-one this year, and I've never seen our State Capitol. I think it is about time." I said, "Would you be willing to give your story about what you did with your life, despite not having a high school diploma?" He said, "I'll tell you, and you can tell them." I said, "Fair enough." I interviewed him and wrote down his story. He came to the Capitol with us.

I also interviewed my mom. She'd never gotten her high school diploma. She was three months from getting it when, during World War II, her parents said it was more important she work, because a lot of her brothers had gone off to war. I had four of my kids before I knew my mom didn't have her high school diploma. She said, "I was afraid if you knew, you would all think you could get away without getting a high school diploma."

I took hers and Buck's testimonies up to the Capitol.

At some point before the hearing, Ruth Lindstrom called me. I had never met her before. I later went to some of the moms meetings at her home. They were really nice social events with dessert and coffee. She'd have different topics. A lot of people came to those.

Ruth had seen my name on the list to testify at this hearing and was wondering what I was going to talk about. I don't remember if I had anything prepared when she called me, because it was literally like two days before the hearing before we had time to prepare.

When we showed up at the hearing, nobody knew who I was. They were all kind of nervous, because they're like "Who are these people? What are they going to say? They could blow this whole thing." I didn't know they were thinking any of that at the time. Ruth was there. So were the folks from HSLDA—Chris Klicka, specifically.

Before the testimonies started, DFL Senator Sandra Pappas said, "We have over four hundred homeschool children out in the hallways, and you would never know it because you could hear a pin drop out there." She said, "If there's ever a testimony that's spoken without words, it's how well all of these kids are behaved, waiting for us in here."

That was how the hearing started, with her acknowledgment of all of those good little kids sitting out there. It was great!

It was Senator Pappas chairing, and she let Erin speak on behalf of the children of homeschool families, which was really unexpected. So we were some of the people that actually got to formally present. I think that was just by God's hand.

When we sat down, Senator Pappas said, "I understand we have a six-year-old homeschool child that wants to tell us something." Erin leaned into the mic and said, "I'm eight." She did not mean it obnoxiously. It was just matter-of-fact correction. But that was a side of Erin I had never met before. Put a mic in front of her and stand back.

Erin:

I don't remember it very well, but I do remember being up there. I had my paper, and I basically just read it. Afterward, as I looked around, there were people just kind of smiling.

Bonnie:

She read her speech, and she did pretty well. I think a lot of the senators' hearts were tweaked that day with "I hadn't really thought about it like that"—that the principle, if taken to its nth degree, would deny an eight-year-old the privilege of teaching a five or six-year-old, and how beautiful that is to have happen in the home.

Erin:

I remember as we were writing it, thinking, in my eight-year-old mind, *If I can do this, then surely someone else shouldn't necessarily have to have a piece of paper, because anyone can teach anyone else.*

Bonnie:

I think she said something like, "I'm pretty good at it."

They let Erin go before me, and when she was done they made a point of saying to me, "You're the last one. We're pretty much out of time."

Erin Erpelding with her mother testifying before the Senate
Education Committee hearing March 21, 2001.
Photo by David J. Oakes

I remember, Senator Kenric Scheevel—ironically, he and I had had some dealings before with my old job. I was a wildlife biologist for the state and managed endangered species. He'd represented trout fishermen who wanted to do something with some stream, and I'd been on the other side. After I was done testifying, Senator Scheevel said, "It sounds to me like this is one of those areas where we need to just leave well enough alone. It sounds like they know what they are doing."

That was his comment, though he prefaced it with sort of a "Kind of funny meeting you here." But the testimony was just over the top with why this was working, and he wholeheartedly agreed. He was all about just giving people the freedom to do what's working—"if it's not broke don't fix it" kind of a thing.

Memories from Homeschooling
Bonnie:

When the kids were little, I gave them a break to go across the street to the park swings. We were always very discreet about playing in the middle of the day. I made sure it was only a fifteen-minute break. We had a homeschool family two houses down and another five blocks away. The kids were all about the same age.

There were probably about five or six of them there, and our local newspaper editor happened to be walking around with his camera. He asked me, "Are you running a daycare?" I said, "No, these are neighbors, and we are homeschool families taking a little break." He pulled out his notebook and said, "Do you mind if I interview the kids?"

He seemed so enthusiastic I made a split-minute decision and said, "I suppose that's okay," taking a risk, because these kids were quite little yet. Of course the first thing he asked my son was "What is your favorite subject?" Ryan said, "Recess." We didn't even use that word. I think Erin told him math, and I thought, *Okay, that's better.*

The guy did this sweet article about the homeschool kids and put big pictures in of each one of them. It was nice. He gave some really good press to it, and over the years he has come to know our family.

We had one instance of a police officer following my son home. It's a small enough town Ryan could ride his bike to the edge of town and gopher trap the ditches. He'd gotten permission to do that, and normally he would do it between seven and eight in the morning. Well, for some reason that morning, it didn't get done. It was after nine o'clock, and he said, "Mom, can I quick go check my gopher traps?"

I said, "No, school's already in session. It's not a good idea." "But Dad said it is good trapping ethic to check it every morning." I said, "All right, go straight there, and come straight back." He must have been at least twelve at the time.

He comes biking home, and here is a squad car following him.

Well, it's about nine forty-five when he gets home, and, totally unusual morning, I'm in the shower.

The police officer, I found out later, had stopped him and said, "Son, how come you're not in school?" Ryan said, "I'm homeschooled." And the officer said, "Do you mind if I call your mom and make sure that she agrees with you on that?"

Well, I'm in the shower, so I didn't hear the phone. So he gets the answering machine. I think it said something like "If you're calling before noon, we're doing school." The officer said, "Well, she's not answering. How about I just come home with you and ask her myself?"

So Ryan is pedaling away, and the officer is driving really slowly behind him. Talk about intimidating. Ryan gets in, and I'm still in the bathroom. He comes, "Mom, you've got to hurry. There is a policeman who wants to talk to you." I said, "What happened?" Ryan said, "He just wants to talk to you." And then he runs back downstairs.

He probably said, "She's in the shower." Because the police officer said, "Tell your mom I will call her in ten minutes."

He did call me ten minutes later, and I confirmed we were homeschooling. The police officer, interestingly enough, was very interested in homeschooling. He asked, "How long have you been doing this?" I said, "We've been homeschooling for about eight or nine years." He said, "Really? I've never seen your kids around town."

I said, "That's good. That means we were successful. Our goal was to never have them out and about in the daytime. You guys have better things to do than trying to figure out who's homeschooled and who isn't—you know, without putting a big label on the back of their heads." He said, "We appreciate that."

After that, if I sent the kids down to the library or somewhere in the middle of the day, I'd write permission slips, which just said, "We're a homeschool family. They are going from here to there, and they will be back at such and such time," so that people would know we weren't just willy-nilly letting these kids run around town. I think that note came in handy only once.

127

Dodge County Homeschooling Association Involvement
Bonnie:

We have been on the Dodge County Homeschooling Association board from about 2001 to the present. I'd been an informal legislative liaison for them. I'd keep them up to date on what was happening with homeschool law and give little blips in our newsletters and at meetings about things to watch for, senators to call, things like that.

Because of my interest in science, I'd do field trips and ended up becoming the activities director. I also teach some science co-op classes.

There was a season where we had moms coming through our house at least twice a week. Sometimes they would just drop in, sometimes it was through co-op class, but then we'd start talking about anything from changing diapers to chore charts and to how to get your kids to eat their vegetables!

And, to be honest, I couldn't have done it without all of those moms. I know some moms that by and large homeschool on their own, and I don't know how they do it. I couldn't have. Almost all of what I know I learned from somebody else. If it wasn't my own mom, it was another mom, some of them even younger than me. I just love that interaction. People say, "How do you homeschool? I could never homeschool." Thinking back, I could never have done it any other way, because I needed the input from other moms and the support to homeschool in such a way that we were all still more or less enjoying ourselves.

I think of non-homeschool moms who are working and juggling homework at night for two hours, and then if they're a Christian household, dealing with evolution and abortion, and how much more stressful that would be.

About 2004, we became active in RAACHE through their choir.

MÂCHÉ Involvement
Bonnie:

We went to MÂCHÉ every time it was in Rochester, and I would say half the time it was at the RiverCentre in St. Paul.

We've never gone to Duluth, but Erin and Ryan have gone there to help.

Erin:

We started volunteering, four years ago maybe, because it was just neat to see other homeschoolers from across the state and some people that you'd meet from various other things. It was great to be able to give back and have fun while you were doing it.

Bonnie:

My husband and I started volunteering at MÂCHÉ probably about five or six years ago to host workshops, or do the security, or the coat check.

Interacting with the School District

Bonnie:

As far as our school district, we haven't really had any issues, but Triton School District (Dodge Center) gave families some grief one year on their reporting and having to bring all of their schoolbooks in and have them approved. However, enough of the members were also HSLDA members that one phone call cleared that up. HSLDA was great that way.

I think the school districts are relieved that they don't have to keep track so much anymore since that new law passed [Mandate Reduction 2011]. I've heard them say, "We don't have anything to do with them anyhow." Still, we have reached out. We have a kickoff picnic every fall, and we've asked the new superintendent to come and judge our pie baking contest. We invite local celebrities, like the mayor or someone, just to introduce people to homeschooling so that they know we don't eat our children at night when no one's looking.

Greatest Moments in Homeschooling

Bonnie:

My first greatest moment in homeschooling was when I figured out I could teach somebody how to read. That might sounds strange because both my husband and I have college degrees, but it scared me because English wasn't my area. Science was. So I really felt like I didn't know if I could do it. I felt like I was experimenting on my kids. So when Erin jumped up out of the couch and said, "I can read!" That was one of those moments I'll never forget.

The other, was twelve years later when she'd actually written for another instructor who had a high standard, and he'd seen her writing as good. It just made me sigh in relief.

It was Erin's first PSEO [Post-Secondary Enrollment Options] class. It was a medical bio-ethics class. She came home and said, "Mom, you have to read these comments."

She'd gotten one hundred percent on the paper, but the teacher had a long column accusing her of proselytizing. He had a high standard for their writing, which is kind of rare nowadays. So I respected him for that.

Her second paper he docked her some points, and I said, "Talk to him. Find out if you got points taken off for legitimate reasons that you need to improve in, or is he just a little steamed now because you're still presenting this conservative Christian viewpoint?"

She walked into his office, and he said, "Erin, I know what you are going to say. You're an evangelical Christian. I'm not worried about you. You're going to get A's in this class." She hadn't even said anything yet. He continued to give her an A, even though she never backed down on presenting her Christian viewpoint.

Erin:

I would love to be able to homeschool. So it's what I'm planning, and I wouldn't be afraid to be involved in the political realm. I haven't done much other than what I've done through my parents. But I think that's the only reason people are able to do what they are doing today, because other people before us went to the Capitol and wrote to their senators and did this stuff. And I'm one of those people. I'm more than willing to get involved in the future and be a voice.

<u>Advice</u>

Bonnie:

A piece of advice that our kids gave us is to keep them in a community of like-minded homeschoolers so that they never feel strange, so that they have a "normal" that isn't that far from them. Whether it's a group of kids playing volleyball or even going on vacations with other like-minded people, our kids said, "That helped us realize there were other people like us out there."

Keep your kids hearts at home—not exclusively, but just keep your finger on the pulse of where their heart is. If you are losing them to a good thing, you are still losing them. We've had to pull out of things when we saw that our child's new friends or cliques start to become their primary focus. Pulling them out is a very painful thing, and doing it gently is hard, because once you see it, it's kind of too late. It's like getting gum out of hair. But, no matter what the thing is that's pulling them away, it isn't worth losing their heart for the Lord.

If you are going to be relaxed in homeschooling, don't let it be in reading. With reading, sooner is better. We stressed reading in our home. Even when they were little and couldn't read, we'd read bedtime stories and series to them.

I know there are some children with learning disabilities where reading isn't easy, but read out loud to them. Be picky and look for stuff that has merit and expands their vocabulary, because reading good authors makes them better writers. Start early. You'll reap the rewards later in life.

Erin:

Keep it simple and make sure that your passion lies first in teaching your children to love the Lord, and then He will supply the rest. But another important thing would be to make learning interesting. Don't start your kids right away on textbooks, so that, by second grade, they already hate school.

Do more engaged learning, where you are actually going out and doing things, so that when your kids are starting high school, they don't already have a distaste for school, because, it's only going to get harder—more book work, more papers, etc. Keep a love for learning in whatever you are teaching. That is probably one of the most important things.

Chapter Twenty

The Bryants participate in a local support group, connect with MÂCHÉ board members, join the MÂCHÉ board of directors, and attend the Senate hearing proposing new homeschool requirements.

Written Contribution Submitted (December 4, 2013) by:
Mac and **Karen Bryant** (Past MÂCHÉ Board Members)
Children: *Luke, Lindsay*

Karen:

I don't recall the exact year we began serving on the MÂCHÉ board of directors, but Mac and I recall praying about "long and short term" goals one year, and interestingly we wrote a goal of serving on the MÂCHÉ board. We were a part of a group of parents in the Alexandria area that organized a formal support group, which still exists, called LEARN at Home.

While being involved in serving through our local support group, we attended a meeting in Iowa with Inge Cannon, who at the time was serving in an official capacity with HSLDA. At that meeting were John and Lynne Cooke, board members for MÂCHÉ, and Dean and Ruth Lindstrom, who eventually became MÂCHÉ board members.

Sometime later, Mac and I received a call from John and Lynne Cooke to visit about MÂCHÉ and our possible interest in serving in the organization. I'm going to guess we joined the board of directors around 1994 or so. (See photo)

2001 Senate Hearing

Karen:

One of my most exciting memories was in March of 2001 when the Minnesota Senate Education Committee held a hearing on a Senate bill that proposed two new regulations on homeschoolers. The bill required home educating parents to 1) have a high school diploma and 2) submit their standardized test scores.

MÂCHÉ Board 2001: Schurkes, von Gohrens,
Bryants, Lindstroms, Cookes

Without getting into details about MÂCHÉ's specific concerns with these two elements of the bill, the fact that unnecessary regulations were being imposed upon homeschooling families was reason enough for MÂCHÉ to lobby against the bill.

The homeschooling community mightily rose to the occasion, and the halls of the Capitol were filled with eight hundred homeschoolers.

There was little room in the committee meeting room, so most families were outside the meeting room or even in halls on other floors. There was a sound system provided for homeschoolers outside the building to listen to the meeting. When arguments were made in favor of home education, cheers could be heard outside the meeting room and began to unnerve some senators.

I recall an individual from the Minnesota Department of Education, testifying in favor of the bill, making the statement that when the original law was written, it was the intention that the standardized test scores be submitted.

Little did she know two of the key crafters of the original legislation were in the room, Senator Gen Olson and MÂCHÉ co-founder and attorney Roger Schurke, who readily took the stand to testify that her interpretation was absolutely false. Roger testified the intent was designed with the opposite in mind, that being to protect the privacy of homeschooling families.

I remember the tension and silence in the room when the testimonies ended and the senators began to cast their votes one by one. I will never forget the sobering realization that flashed through my mind at that moment—our freedoms could be taken away in the blink of an eye. It makes me wonder how the next generation will respond to threats to homeschooling that may loom in the future.

It's awesome to think that the victory that occurred at the Capitol on March 21, 2001, is being enjoyed by home educators today.

Another piece of information worth noting from that hearing twelve years ago is that Senator Steve Kelley argued the point that parents participating in government-funded virtual schools must obviously be seeking the support and guidance of the government school systems, and he quickly lumped privately-funded and parent-directed home educators in with government-funded virtual schooling families. He then suggested there should be no question that homeschoolers should submit their test scores to the government schools from which home educators seek to use services.

Ministering at MÂCHÉ

Karen:

Another fond memory I have is praying for a "divine appointment" with a home educating parent at the MÂCHÉ conference in Rochester. At the end of the conference, I was at the Support Group booth and saw a mother standing on the edge of the crowd around the parents, seeking answers to homeschooling questions. I made a point to speak with her and found she was carrying such a huge burden for her children and family at the time. We visited and prayed, and I knew it was a moment anointed by the Lord.

At a subsequent conference, this woman and I saw each other again, and I had the opportunity to be blessed by her praise report of how God had intervened in her marriage, in the family's finances, and in their family life over the past year.

God's faithfulness in the lives of parents who are seeking to serve Him and raise their children to know, love, and serve the living God is amazing, and His blessing upon this lifestyle that defies the ways of the world is undeniable.

Favorite Memories

Mac:

Here are some of my memories of our time spent with the MÂCHÉ board

- Meeting at John and Lynne Cooke's house, always having pizza for dinner, and then watching Roger very unselfconsciously stretch out on the floor as the meeting grew looooong.
- Watching Ruth Lindstrom pour herself a cup of coffee and cradle it in her hands, making it look like the very best coffee in the world!
- Listening to the kind but extremely convincing words of Chris Klicka during a Minnesota Home Education Senate hearing. I marveled at how Chris could be so gentle and so humble with his words, yet portray such overwhelming wisdom without alienating the opposition.
- Getting a kick out of hearing John Tuma's penchant for summing up issues in a very convincing manner, even if I disagreed with his position.
- Watching my wife, Karen, intensely shop at the curriculum fair and share her considerable wisdom at the Veteran's booth with other homeschool moms.
- Observing Roger Schurke get the crowd involved at a MÂCHÉ conference general meeting: "Okay, who is wearing two different colors of socks?" "Now, who has not washed his

socks for two days or more?" "Who has the most kids? Six? Eight? Ten? Okay, twelve kids wins!"

- Watching the newer home school parents be overwhelmed (like I was) the first year at the curriculum fair! "Yikes! It is so big! So much to pick from! Where do I start?"
- One of the great memories of conferences was watching the dads tenderly care for their little ones. I could see God working through them—knowing their legacies would be great.
- Talking with David Watkins, one-on-one, and seeing his gentleness and his pastor's heart.

Chapter Twenty-One

John Tuma is approached by Amy Klobuchar, who wants to alter the charge of truancy in the Compulsory Attendance Law from a misdemeanor to a petty misdemeanor. John gladly agrees.

Interview (December 1, 2012) with:
John Tuma (MÂCHÉ's Legislative Liaison and MÂCHÉ Board Member)
> Wife: *Wendy (MÂCHÉ Board Member)*
> Children: *Cal, Molly*

<u>Changing the Law to a Petty Misdemeanor</u>
John:

Before 2002, under the law it's written that, if anyone violates the provisions of the homeschool law, it's a misdemeanor. It's a crime, and you can go to jail for up to ninety days and be fined a couple of thousand dollars.

But in 2002, County Attorney Amy Klobuchar came to me and explained: We want to do this program for habitual truants, the guys hanging out on corners doing drugs. We want to deal with them under our child protection statutes before there is any criminal process, so we're trying to de-criminalize a lot of this activity. But there is a glitch. The public defender is saying if we bring this claim of habitual truancy, which is the easiest way to get to these drug dealer kids (It's easier to show they've missed seven days of school than to show they are out dealing drugs.) the problem is, the minute we claim they're habitually truant, we violate the statute in the Compulsory Attendance Law.

What she wanted to do was turn violating the Compulsory Attendance Law into a petty misdemeanor—a parking ticket. I went "Sounds good to me." I worked alongside Stanek [IR representative], who was one of the authors of this big bill. It covered lots of issues, and I managed to slip in there provisions making violating the law a petty misdemeanor. Talk about slipping things into a big bill in the late of night. This was a thousand-page bill, and we slipped in what looked like a very innocuous provision, essentially only adding the word "petty."

So now the most a school district can do is fine parents; they can't send them to jail. We did this very quietly, and to anybody who questioned it, we'd say, "Amy Klobuchar supports this."

So because of Amy Klobuchar wanting her program for druggie kids, I was able to basically make violating the Compulsory Attendance Law a petty misdemeanor.

Chapter Twenty-Two

The Wetjens begin homeschooling in 1986 and become faithful MÂCHÉ volunteers. Their involvement with MÂCHÉ continues to the present.

Written Contribution Submitted (December 24, 2013) by: John Wetjen and **Doris Wetjen** (MÂCHÉ Administrative Director)
Children: *one son, one daughter*

John and Doris:

We were introduced to the idea of homeschooling by Dr. Raymond and Dorothy Moore on Dr. Dobson's program in the early 1980s. After considerable prayer, we felt the Lord was calling us to homeschool. We began homeschooling in 1986, and with God's help, we home educated both of our children from kindergarten through high school.

We all loved to read. When our kids were little, every evening, it was "Daddy, *weed* to us." We read out loud every Hardy Boys book ever written, at least twice, and numerous other books. During our children's elementary years, we didn't have television. On our trips to the library, our kids would max out their cards and ours, as well, and bring home as many as eighty books! When it was time to return the books, they had read them all!

A friend of ours had one of the first personal computers on the market—a Commodore 64. He invited our son to try it out. Being a kinesthetic learner, he took to it like a duck to water! We ordered a computer with a "huge" 30-megabyte hard drive from a company in Texas, but we couldn't figure out how to set it up or make it work, so we sent it back. Then we visited a newly opened local computer store and discovered that computers now had 40-megabyte hard drives. We couldn't believe how fast the computer market was changing! The operating system was DOS and came with a dot matrix printer. The educational software we bought came on 7.5 inch floppy discs. Instructions included manual settings to the auto exec bat file, indicating buffer numbers and typing in some DOS code. Soon our son was reading big, thick computer manuals and was teaching us about the complexity of hard drives, how to access local BBS (bulletin board services) and go online to the library to reserve books for checkout.

In addition to learning the required subjects, homeschooling allowed our children to pursue their interests in depth. Our daughter had an interest in fabrics and creative crafts. She spent time with her grandmother, who taught her how to weave rugs on a loom, make crazy-patch quilt blocks, and create her own sewing patterns.

MÂCHÉ Involvement
John and Doris:

We were involved with MÂCHÉ from its inception, renewed our membership every year, and attended the conferences. We volunteered our time and talents at the conferences, helping with everything from the used book sale and onsite registration to setting up the first coat and book check. As our kids got older, they volunteered at the conference, as well. Throughout the year we helped with commencement, the handbook, and other projects.

Greatest Lessons from Homeschooling Years
John and Doris:

We discovered that we were not the "perfect" homeschooling family, mostly because we were not perfect parents. On more than one occasion, while we would be praying for our children and asking God to work in their lives, the Holy Spirit would show us an area in our own lives that was not pleasing to God! When our sin affected our children (such as not showing them the respect that we'd want to be shown if we were the kids and they were the parents), the Holy Spirit impressed upon us that we needed to confess our sin to our children and ask for their forgiveness. It was humbling but also a blessing to be told, "Oh, I've known for quite a while that you had that problem of being disrespectful toward me. I was wondering when God was going to talk to you about that. Sure, I forgive you!" God showed us that our children were learning how to receive instruction and correction from God, and how to confess sin and ask for forgiveness, by seeing us do that. As our children moved toward adulthood, we were so blessed to hear them talk about the ministry of the Holy Spirit in their personal relationship with their Heavenly Father through our Lord Jesus Christ.

As parents homeschooling our children, we learned more fully the meaning of Psalm 127:1: "Except the Lord build the house, they labor in vain that build it . . ." Our efforts alone were not sufficient to produce godly children. Like us, they needed their own personal relationship with the Lord Jesus Christ and the indwelling Holy Spirit to work in them "both to will and to do His good pleasure" (Philippians 2:13). We have been extremely blessed to see God's love for our son and daughter, and His blessing on their lives. Now that they're happily married and have homes of their own, we continue to say, "Being confident of this very thing, that He which hath begun a good work in (us and in our children) will perform it until the day of Jesus Christ" (Philippians 1:6).

Advice

John and Doris:

Pray. Ask God for wisdom. Your child is uniquely made by God. Find out what God is leading you to do in the raising of your child, and then follow that. God is wiser than any man. Don't look to man for wisdom—look to God. Pray that your children will receive Jesus as their personal Lord and Savior. Then teach your children, from an early age, to pray and ask God for His wisdom for their lives. You will not always be with your children. They need to know how to hear from God for themselves. You cannot be the Holy Spirit to your children. They have to have the Holy Spirit in their own lives.

Patience. There is a certain amount of patience that is required. Homeschooling is definitely not about rushing through. Realize that the same principle of agriculture is operating in your home. You are going to sow, water, and nourish, and there will be various seasons where you will reap some results. But the final harvest will not take place until eternity. We have to do everything with a view to eternity. "Does what I'm doing today have a practical end in eternity?"

Chapter Twenty-Three

The Watkinses begin homeschooling the year after the Compulsory Attendance Law has been ruled unconstitutionally vague and while a new law has not yet been passed. The Cookes ask for their help with MÂCHÉ, and they start volunteering during MÂCHÉ conferences. They join the MÂCHÉ board of directors and are put in charge of the conferences. David becomes chairman of MÂCHÉ's working board and then executive director when MÂCHÉ eventually shifts to a policy board.

Interview (August 7, 2013 & December 2, 2013) with:
David Watkins (Executive Director of MÂCHÉ)
Linda Watkins (MÂCHÉ Conference Director)
        Children: *Paul, Rebecca, John, Elisabeth, Daniel, Timothy, Sara, Philip*

Linda:

    We first started homeschooling the summer of 1986, mostly due to one of our daughters who we knew had some hearing problems since birth. However, two years before that was when David first began asking me what I thought about home educating our children. My thoughts at that time were that only professional teachers could successfully teach children to read, and I had no training. So I said I didn't think we should home educate.

    When our daughter was four, we received a notice from our school district that we needed to take her in for preschool screening. Thinking that we were required by law to do this and trying to be good citizens, we took her to the screening.

    They said she had a hearing loss, which we already knew, and recommended that we put her in a summer school program for children who had learning issues. Still not knowing we were not required to do that, we did so.

The teachers were very kind and easy to work with, so we had no complaints against the teachers or what they taught, but the other students who attended the program had significantly different issues than our daughter. Some were violent. Some had emotional issues. Our daughter simply had hearing loss. The program did not meet her needs.

At the end of the summer, the teachers said that our daughter had some other learning issues above her hearing loss and needed one-on-one help. They recommended she be put into special classes in the public school. We did not want to put her in special classes. Since our older children were in Christian school, we enrolled her in first grade there, intending to work at home with her to help her stay caught up with the other students. The school tried to find a teacher who would be available to help with remedial lessons, but it just didn't work out very well.

We had been hearing about home education, but we had always just brushed it off because I didn't think I could do it. We now began to think more seriously about going that direction. We thought, *The public school told us she needs one-on-one help, and the Christian school isn't working out well. We might as well homeschool.*

The home education program we chose wanted us to homeschool the whole family, so we took the older children out of Christian school and started home educating them all.

The younger children were okay with the transition. They just wanted to do whatever we said. It was hardest for our oldest son, who was going into eighth grade. He was pretty peer-dependent and into sports and was afraid he was going to miss out on something he enjoyed.

We enrolled him in community sports, so he could participate in something besides academics. At the end of that year, he saw some of his old friends at the Christian school and told us, "Boy, am I glad we homeschooled. There's a difference between my old friends and me."

The Law
Linda:

We didn't really think about whether or not homeschooling was legal; we just assumed it was. Later, David heard the law was very vague and was being rewritten. That was the first we knew that it wasn't "legal," but it wasn't "illegal" either.

That first year, the marching band from the nearby middle school would march down our street during school hours. Our kids loved it. They would run to the window and watch. I thought, *Well, as long as they stand back, no one will see them.* One day, all the kids in the band started waving at them. I thought, *Oh no! Now they know we are homeschooling!* I felt so illegal.

After we had been homeschooling for a while, we found out there was a lady nearby who homeschooled. Then we discovered that a friend of David's parents, Lynn Wilson, who had just moved to Minnesota, was homeschooling and had been down at the Capitol during the hearings.

Even after they passed the new law, I was very hesitant to take the children outside during school hours or go shopping with them. I didn't want people asking questions or getting us arrested or something. We had heard that even grandparents and neighbors were reporting homeschool children as truant. As the years went by and more people began to know about homeschooling and its legality, we began to be more and more open with it.

David:

When we started home educating in 1986, we were pretty open with the school district. We were in Anoka-Hennepin District 11, which at that time was very antagonistic toward homeschooling, but we didn't have any trouble with the superintendent, Dr. Lew Finch, or anyone else in the district.

In all the years we home educated, we only had one home visit. The man was a retired principal, an older gentleman, nice fellow. I stayed home from work that day, and he was here about thirty minutes or so. After we chatted, I said, "Would you like to see our lesson plans or our curriculum?" He said, "No. I can see just by talking to you people that you have everything together just fine."

Because I knew there were others who maybe wouldn't have the same standards as we did, I offered to him, "If you have some homeschoolers who need help, I would be happy to be a liaison and help you work with them." I tried to be very open and helpful so that they knew we didn't have an ax to grind. We just felt like we could do a better job educating our children than the public school or the private school.

Besides that, another wonderful benefit of homeschooling was that our children enjoyed each other and were friends. Our children had snowball fights, played army, taught each other how to ride bikes, and were on ball teams together. The family time and togetherness were really good.

Linda:

One of my favorite memories of those early days of homeschooling was when I taught our fifth child to read. I thought teaching reading was something only a professional teacher could do. I had no idea how to do it, but I got phonics resources from A Beka Books and taught him his phonics rules. He then began putting the sounds together. Before Christmas that year, he was reading short verses out of the Bible, and I thought, *He's reading, and I taught him!* I was so thrilled.

He was our first fully home-educated child. He joined the marines several years ago and had to take the ASVAB Test (Armed Services Vocational Aptitude Battery). I felt like this was a test of my teaching skills, and I was very nervous. He got a score of ninety-five on the test out of a possible ninety-nine, and he said, "And, Mom, the average test score is around thirty-five." He had aced it, and all I could think of was *I passed!*

Another favorite memory happened just a few years ago at the conclusion of a year-long support group that I was teaching called Smoothing the Way. I asked the ladies to share the one most important thing that they each had learned during the year about home educating their children. One lady raised her hand and said something like the following: "When my children were in public school, one child would go to one class or activity and another child would always be going to a different class and activity. They never seemed to be doing anything together, and our family never saw each other in the same place at the same time for very long. We rarely even had dinner together. Now that we've been homeschooling for eight months, my children are best friends and have learned to work and play together. Best of all, we now feel like a family. Thank you for teaching me how to do this!"

Before joining MÂCHÉ, our main resource for advice and curriculum was the Advanced Training Institute (ATI), which offered an annual national conference and supplied us with our curriculum. We would get supplemental materials from other suppliers, but we couldn't get the answer booklets. The publishers would not give us the answer keys, because we were not certified teachers. I had to figure the material out with my kids, which was time-consuming, but we did have curriculum and a conference once a year.

When MÂCHÉ was having their first conference, our friend Lynn Wilson invited us to attend, but we didn't go because I didn't have time. I was too busy homeschooling five kids and three preschoolers. It was several years later that I learned how deceptive that excuse really was. I learned some of my best teaching tips from the annual conferences, which would have been such tremendous help if I'd only learned them sooner.

Several years later when we attended an ATI conference in Oklahoma City, we were walking through the halls looking at people's name tags to see where they were from, and we saw Minnesota, then Minnesota, and then Minnesota. I called out, "Minnesota! You're from Minnesota and you homeschool?" That was when we met John and Lynne Cooke. They were very friendly. They kind of took us under their wings after that and would occasionally call us and ask us how we were doing. They have a real gift with mentoring people and have been such a blessing to so many.

MÂCHÉ Involvement

Linda:

The first MÂCHÉ conference we attended was at Crystal Evangelical Free Church in 1991. In the spring of 1993, the Cookes called us and said they'd like to talk to us about helping them with the MÂCHÉ conference. We liked them so well and they had encouraged us so much in the past that we said that we would do it.

Later, the Cookes put us in charge of organizing the hosts and hostesses. I do not like to be in front of people, so I assisted, making phone calls to the volunteers and doing the behind-the-scenes work. Once we got to the conference, David took it from there. That was nice because then I could attend the workshops.

The Cookes were a big help to us in getting this organized. There were lots of good people who were willing to help and also wonderful speakers at the conferences. We did that for nine years.

David:

I enjoyed working with people and seeing what God was doing as the homeschool movement grew. We began to be consistently involved with the MÂCHÉ conference on an annual basis.

After several years, I think our interest in pursuing and promoting home education must have caught the MÂCHÉ board's attention. Our children helped us at the conference. I think our children making wise decisions was a good testimony for what can happen when you home educate with Christ as the focus. When there was an opening on the MÂCHÉ board, we were asked if we would be interested in the position.

Linda:

They asked us in 2001 to join the board. We prayed and talked about it a lot and decided it was not something we could do. David was a pastor, had a second job, and we were just too busy to do anything else.

David:

I felt perhaps we needed to be involved to help the next generation, but I said, "Okay, if Linda's not interested, I don't want to go that direction either, because we need to be unified."

Linda:

The following year, we were at the Saturday night banquet for the volunteers, after coordinating the hosts and hostesses, and I felt God telling me, "You need to do this." So I leaned over and told David, "I think we need to join the board."

He did a double take. "What? You said we didn't have time." I said, "Yes, and we still don't have the time, but I just really feel we need to be doing this." He said, "I don't know if they still want us." I said, "Well, go ask the Cookes." We were close enough friends that they wouldn't be offended if we asked them.

David:

I asked John Cooke and Roger Schurke if the board member position was still open. They said, "Yes, it is." I had reminded Linda what she had told me the year before about us not having time. But Linda had now grasped the vision, so I said, "We would reconsider an invitation if the board felt that they wanted us."

Joining the MÂCHÉ Board of Directors

David:

We interviewed with the board probably a month later. They already knew us because of the conference, so we weren't new material. We answered questions and made sure they knew where we were coming from, and we made sure we understood where the board was coming from.

I wanted them to know I had a pastor's heart, and that was my calling. Our motivation to join the board was the home education discipleship of children for Christ. The board was in agreement, so we said, "Okay."

They extended a formal invitation to us at that point, and, in the fall of 2002, we joined the MÂCHÉ board, and God rearranged our time to make it work.

Put in Charge of the MÂCHÉ Conferences
Linda:

We had to miss the first board meeting because of a previous engagement. While we were absent from the meeting, the board voted to put us in charge of the conference. It shocked us, because the conference was such a big event and we were the newbies on the board, but the work was right down my alley and I enjoyed it.

The first MÂCHÉ conference that we directed was in the spring of 2003. Ruth Lindstrom, Karen Bryant, and the Cookes previously had put the conferences together as a group effort. Then Carla Biederman, no longer on the board but who had agreed to help plan the conferences, began coordinating the conferences. She had much of the preparation for the next conference already in motion when we came on the board, and she spent a great deal of time teaching me the tricks of the trade as we worked together. Because of Carla, we really didn't have the whole load that first year, so thankfully it was easy to slip into place and take over.

David:

The next year, 2004, Roger and Merryl decided that they would step down. Roger wanted someone with a legal mind to be on the board, and John Tuma fit that bill.

John and Wendy Tuma joined the board the year after we did. Once they were there, Roger felt more comfortable stepping back from the board, and I was recommended for chairman.

I served as chairman for seven years. In 2011, the board decided to move from a working board to a policy board with an executive director. I became MÂCHÉ's first executive director.

Favorite Aspects of MÂCHÉ
David:

I enjoy hearing the testimonies of people whose lives have been impacted by a MÂCHÉ conference, a keynote speaker, or an exhibitor. We have seen people led to Christ at the conference, and that's exciting. It's a joy to know we've maybe had a part in that, whether it's through our prayer, planning, or something else.

To watch God touch someone's life and then to see those same people coming back year after year, that's exciting. You get to see them go through the commencement ceremony with their children and then watch those graduates go out and make a positive difference in the world.

MÂCHÉ Graduations
David:

The graduation is one of the faces of MÂCHÉ. A lot of people who attend commencements don't home educate. Maybe they have even been antagonistic to home education, but because they have a relative or friend who is home educating, they come and are impressed. We get comments every year from people saying, "This was well done. I was impressed with the young people, with their testimonies, their music, and their displays."

MÂCHÉ doesn't actually do the graduating. We provide the mechanism, which gives parents a platform from which to graduate their children. So it's the individual homeschool families on stage. You get to watch parents hand that diploma to their son or daughter and give all the hugs. It's very moving.

It's really a ministry, and it's a joy to be part of it. We've had a great variety of commencement speakers, from pastors and missionaries to elected officials. We take speaker recommendations from the students, and we process those. If one fits the bill, then we pray and contact them. Every year we have good speakers from a variety of different places.

Colleges
Linda:

When we first began homeschooling, we did not encourage our kids to go on to college because sometimes colleges, even "Christian" colleges, can have a negative impact on students' character and convictions. However, several of our kids wanted to go into professions that required a four-year degree. So we interviewed colleges.

We wanted to know if the colleges believed the same way we did, and we were very picky. Five of our kids went on to college of one sort or another, and two started their own businesses.

The Next Generation
Linda:

We have sixteen grandchildren. I didn't want our children to feel like they had to homeschool because we were involved with MÂCHÉ. They, however, had their own vision of homeschooling their families. They wanted to do it, and they enjoy it. Those who are married, married fellow homeschool students. With both Mom and Dad having been homeschooled, it was easier for them because they knew what to expect.

Advice

David:

Keep that support network so you know you are not alone. There are a lot of support mechanisms around, including the annual MÂCHÉ conferences, and they are critical to help the homeschool parents be refreshed, whether they are new or have been at it for a number of years.

Linda:

You can do it. I didn't think I could teach my children because I wasn't a professional teacher. Our fifth child was my first homeschool student to teach from kindergarten all the way through high school. When he began reading on his own, I was ecstatic. Anyone can homeschool. If you don't think you're smart enough, learn right along with your kids. It will encourage all of you. You can do this.

David:

Keep a generational view, because homeschooling is an investment. It's not a quick-fix scheme. Keep a focus on eternity and not just on the temporal things.

Linda:

When I homeschooled, I had no idea that people learn differently. I thought everyone learned like I did. Every new homeschool parent should go to a class on learning styles and teaching styles. It just opened a whole new world to me.

David:

I would encourage parents to not be afraid to have children or to home educate with a number of children. Some people can't have a lot of children, and that's fine. But I think those who could and choose not to shortchange themselves.

Our culture tries to program us that one or two children is all a couple should have, but that is a skewed view of the Bible and causes parents to lose potential opportunities and joy. My children are a legacy I can leave for Christ.

Before I got saved, I didn't want children. I wasn't sure that I even wanted to get married. My secular mind asked, *Why bring children into this terrible world?* When I trusted Jesus Christ as my Savior, it changed my view one hundred percent. Christian home education helps parents disciple their children for Christ and gives their children a biblical worldview so they can make a difference for the Lord in the culture around them.

Linda:

Both David and I have such a burden for young families to have Christian mentors to take them under their wings and help them along, whether it's in home education, parenting, health, or other family issues. They can learn from our experiences, and we can help them keep focused in Scripture, where the answers to their issues can be readily found.

David:

The most important advice that we can give is to begin each morning with Scripture reading and prayer with your family. On the days we missed doing that, our days seemed to fall apart no matter how well prepared we were in other ways. The days we spent that time together around God's Word were much more productive.

Chapter Twenty-Four

The Bjorkmans begin homeschooling after it's legal and, while attending MÂCHÉ, learn that Heppner and Heppner Construction is for sale. They buy the business and continue to carry on the Heppner's legacy of supplying eclectic Christian curriculum to homeschoolers across the country.

Written Contribution Submitted (December 2, 2013) by: Brad and **Nancy Bjorkman** (Heppner's Legacy Homeschool Resources)

Children: *Kristina, Katie, Kelsey, Dane*

Nancy:

I began as a homeschool skeptic until 1988, when I had the opportunity to teach in a small homeschool enrichment program. There were twelve or so students, including several grade levels and multiple sibling groups; they gave me a glimpse of what homeschooling could be. They were creative, interactive with all ages, academically adept, and very delightful.

When our daughter entered kindergarten, I realized that I really missed the family time and flexibility we had before school took over our lives. So, for first grade, we decided to give homeschooling a try . . . for one year. One year turned to two and so on until homeschooling became a lifestyle, not just an educational choice.

In January 2006, Brad was laid off from his work of seventeen years. After several wonderful yet unfruitful interviews in the medical community, he had become discouraged.

However, he was for the first time actually available to attend the homeschool conference. It was his first up-close and personal taste of the homeschooling community, and he saw me in what had been "my world" for fifteen years.

Buying Heppner and Heppner Construction
Nancy:

We also learned at MÂCHÉ that Heppner and Heppner Construction (a homeschool resource business) was moving into a new season of their own. Brad and I began to brainstorm about whether God might have a very different direction for the life of our family; that maybe He had been preparing us for years in our skills and passions to do something new.

In May, after a long phone call between Miriam Heppner and I, we felt that it might be a great fit for us to purchase and carry on the Heppner tradition.

That transition was completed in January 2007, and we opened the doors of our store in Elk River, Minnesota, that summer. Ever since, God has done amazing things.

It has been so very exciting to watch Him continue to direct everything that Heppner's Legacy has become. We know that every person who walks through our door is there for a reason. It is then our part to minister to whatever needs He has sent. What an overwhelming privilege and responsibility.

Favorite Memory
Nancy:

My favorite memory was the year that I thought I was the worst homeschool mom ever. My birthday was in the spring, so I'd had all year to be thinking this way. For my birthday, my four kids had collaborated to create a "scroll" that was titled "101 Reasons Mommy has NOT Failed as a Homeschool Mother." I cried as I read through it. It has now been reprinted and framed and hangs in the shop.

Some of the highlights [from the scroll] included:
- Your kids can do their own laundry.
- Our tendency to produce unscheduled team-building activities (like building trebuchets in the family room).
- We know what a trebuchet is.

- Your children fight over Diana Waring tapes.
- Ar (our) spel(l)ing and gra~~me~~(mma)r ar(e) ~~perfict~~ perfect.
- Kelsey looks forward to you leaving the house so that she can clean it.
- Katie is teaching the dog to track.
- Kristina can define, create, and use a thesis statement.
- Check out some of Dane's models (wow!).
- Your children crave conversations with people of another worldview.
- Your husband thinks you're gorgeous.
- Note who your children's heroes are.
- Your children could not only survive but thrive on *Frontier House*.
- Your children laugh together and mean it.
- Your four children also successfully share one bathroom.
- We read by choice.
- Your children know how to learn.

Chapter Twenty-Five

Informed of an opportunity to keep new requirements from being placed upon Minnesota's homeschoolers while at the same time possibly reducing current requirements, John Tuma pursues a bill with the help of Senator Gen Olson and attorney Mike Donnelly of HSLDA.

Interview (December 1, 2012) with:

John Tuma (MÂCHÉ's Legislative Liaison and MÂCHÉ Board Member)

        Wife: *Wendy (MÂCHÉ Board Member)*

        Children: *Cal, Molly*

Mandate Reduction Bill
John:

Often the state sees something happening at the local level and doesn't like it. So they create a mandate saying, "You've got to do this," and now the local unit of government has a mandate and no extra money to do the additional work.

Because of this, there is a constant conflict over the need to reduce mandates. The game is—I do this for a living, and I've played from both sides—the local government says, "We've a practice now that is much better than the mandate you gave us twenty years ago. Can we get rid of this mandate?" It's usually the local officials who complain, and a lot of times the legislature comes back and says, "Well, give us a list."

Often the local officials are reluctant to give a list though, because whatever mandate they'd like removed was probably put in place by some special interest group who'll get mad if it's changed. So local officials often want the legislature to take the heat and create the list, and vice versa.

158

It's kind of like playing hot potato: "No, you do it." "No, you." So in the end, mandates keep piling up, but on occasion a list is made, and the legislature finds the least objectionable mandates and gets rid of those.

Four years ago the school boards called the bluff and came up with a list of mandates to reduce, and on that list was an innocuous little statement, something along the lines of "Improve homeschool reporting requirements."

I was totally unaware of it, but lobbyist Grace Swabe, a former senator who I got along with quite well, caught me in the hall the first day of session and, handing me the list, said, "John, just so you know, you're on this list." Of course, I panicked, because the last thing I wanted was to have lobbyists for the superintendents of school boards writing homeschool law.

My defensive strategy was to introduce our own bill, which I didn't really think would pass (it was a DFL Senate and House). I just didn't want any Democrats to get the idea they could run roughshod over us. So I went to Gen Olson first, and of course Gen Olson said, "Absolutely, I'll take command of this."

I had also heard through the grapevine that Marsha Swails [DFL representative], an award-winning school teacher and newly-elected freshman Democrat, had a liberal campaign manager, Athene Johnson, who was a homeschooler. I went to her, saying, "Would you introduce a bill, our bill for homeschool mandate reduction?"

Once I got them to agree to do a bill, I went to the authors of the bigger mandate reduction bill. I said, "Guys, these two senators want to do something just on this one line. Can you take that provision out of your bill?" They both agreed.

It's really one of those God things. I cannot take credit for it. I was just responding to what was happening around me. Things just kept falling into place. People were like "Oh yeah, definitely, if Marsha Swails wants to do it, I'm not going to touch it." And "Well, if it's Gen Olson. Gen Olson knows this stuff better than anybody else. So yeah, let her carry the bill."

We went through hearings in both the House and the Senate. That first year, we got a few minor things in the House bill (the education omnibus bill), and Gen Olson got her whole package in the Senate bill. She and LeRoy Stumpf, who was the chair of the Education Committee, were good friends, and he put all of her stuff in there.

I actually got our stuff into the final draft of the legislation, but unfortunately the Republicans and the Democrats were at war, and they passed a bare-bones bill—no policy, just the money to fund the schools—as just an "In your face, Tim Pawlenty." They wanted Governor Pawlenty to veto an education bill. Pawlenty surprised them and signed it, and our provision disappeared. So we were left at the altar by mistake.

We didn't really expect it to pass. It was really a defensive action, but Gen Olson surprised us and slipped it into another bill. And it failed again, in almost the exact same scenario. The governor and legislature could not agree, so it didn't happen. After getting close twice with the homeschool mandate reduction bill, I told Gen Olson after the 2010 session that I was pretty much done fighting for the bill. We had successfully used it as a defense tactic to protect us from the superintendents' proposals over the last two years, and that was good enough.

Fortunately, the Lord had other plans. The 2010 election swung big for the Republicans, and for the first time in forty years the Republicans took control of the Senate. That meant Gen Olson was in line to be chair of education for the 2011 session and in a far more powerful position to make the homeschool mandate reduction happen.

The fact that after a long and illustrious career Gen had the honor and opportunity to be chair of that committee was a big deal. In addition, she let everybody know early on that this was going to be her last two years in the legislature. Therefore, this was her legacy opportunity, and one of the top things she wanted to work on out of a hundred different things that she could've picked was passage of the homeschool mandate reduction bill.

Mary Kiffmeyer, a homeschool mom and homeschool pioneer, authored the bill in the House.

As we got closer to final passage of the omnibus education bill that included our homeschool mandate reduction legislation in the 2011 session, the governor's commissioner of education balked at some of the changes we were making regarding the testing mandate. The commissioner actually wanted to go in a more controlling direction for the department where they would tell us what test we could use. This was unacceptable, and Gen skillfully worked out a compromise where we just removed our small positive changes to the testing provisions and kept the rest of the bill intact. Therefore, the final bill that was passed included substantial positive changes, but just nothing regarding testing.

No longer could superintendents make annual visits, and they could not dictate to us what was an appropriate level of education. Superintendents essentially just became keepers of the annual report from homeschoolers, and if they found a violation, it just amounted to a petty misdemeanor due to changes made a decade earlier.

The requirement that some parents had to file annual report cards was deleted. There were also several changes to other minor provisions of homeschooling law that made it easier for homeschooling parents when filling out their annual report, filing immunization records, and going through the driver's license provisions for their teenagers.

Chapter Twenty-Six

Senator Gen Olson leaves a legacy for Minnesota's children, stemming from her passion for literacy. She also helps reduce a number of requirements for Minnesota's homeschoolers.

Interview (January 22, 2013) with:
Senator Gen Olson (A Friend of Homeschoolers)

The Literacy Bill
Gen:

In the reception room at three o'clock in the afternoon on Sunday, after that shut down, we were finally going to get down to work, and I said, "You know, Governor Dayton [DFL, 2011-], I have served through five governors of all parties: Democratic-Farmer-Labor [DFL]; Independent-Republican [IR]; and Independent [I]. Each one has placed a very high value on education."

I said, "You look back to Governor Perpich [DFL, 1983-1991]; he had a very strong legacy for what he did in education and the leadership he took on Open Enrollment and Post-Secondary Enrollment Options, which have now taken off across the country. We were the first in the nation to do it. He also started some of the work on chartering. Arne Carlson [IR, 1991-1999] will be remembered as the one who signed the bill that got chartering going. We were again the first in the nation to have charter schools." Then I said, "I want to skip Ventura [I, 1999-2003]."

He laughed. I said, "Governor Pawlenty [IR, 2003-2011] is going to be remembered, I think, for Q-Comp [the Quality Compensation Bill that made student achievement a factor in compensating teachers as well as investing in staff development for teachers]."

I said, "I don't know what you want to have as your legacy, but in our bill we have something that will be the first in the nation again. It is awarding achievement with our funding and having a funding stream tied to the students achieving proficiency in reading by third grade. That hasn't been done before and is in our literacy package." I just briefly described it.

He piped up and said, "Well, that would be your legacy." I said "Well, no. Not unless you sign it, and I would be more than happy to have it be your legacy." He came back, and he had the literacy package first on his list.

Governor Dayton went all over the state promoting literacy. And more often than not, he's also given me credit for that, but he has taken the stand for it.

If we can just keep building on that, we can get more and more kids reading proficiently by third grade. I just thank the Lord for this.

I've always said, "If you can read, nothing can be withheld from you. If you can't read, someone else will always control what you may access." This greatly affects matters of faith. You know, in the beginning was the Word. And God speaks not only through His Son, the Word, but the written word. And if you can't read it, it undermines the ability of your faith to grow.

The 2011 Mandate Reduction Bill
Gen:

For several years, I worked with John Tuma trying to give mandate relief to our schools. John felt that some of these homeschool reporting requirements (mandates) were burdensome not just to the homeschooling families but also to the superintendents. We took a broad perspective on it and worked with the superintendents group, the county attorneys, and the Department of Motor Vehicle services. Why would a superintendent have to sign off on the study for taking the driver's test? The parent can verify the child has done the study, and the child still has to pass the tests.

In education, we end up rolling bills together, either in one big omnibus bill or a policy bill and funding bill. In cases where you had one party leadership in the legislature and the other party governor, they didn't always agree. We had some of that; if they didn't get their way, they were absolutely not going to sign off on it. Some of those pieces were left in, and the governor vetoed the bill. That happened a couple of times. Usually you go back, iron that out, and send through what was agreed on so you get something, but we went a couple of years with nothing, because there was no bending whatsoever on the part of the chair over on the House side.

In 2011, after the shutdown, we were working to get some of our policy pieces done, and there were a couple things John Tuma worked through and said, "I think we can live without that." We pared it down but still had some significant changes in terms of those areas of required reporting.

I won't go into the details of the conversations at three o'clock in the morning when we were trying to wrap the final education bill up, but it was one of the last things. The commissioner was still holding out against mandate relief for homeschools, and I made it quite clear and said, "If I were you, Commissioner, I wouldn't be picking a fight with me."

It stayed in, and the bill passed.

The commissioner, bless her heart, feels like she's somehow responsible for all the children in the state, and I said, "Commissioner, no, the parents are." I said, "Yes, we have laws, and you have responsibility for our public schools. But until we get things straightened out within our public schools, I wouldn't be spending a lot of time worrying about the homeschoolers."

Advice

Gen:

The charge I would make to homeschoolers is, don't get comfortable. You are an exceptional group in terms of staying engaged with the political process, not only learning it, but learning to know who the players are. Whether it's engaging in their campaign or being sure they understand who you are and what you are doing, it is important to be known by them so that you can call on them. I don't think there is a legislator there who doesn't have homeschool families they know, and sometimes members of their own family. It's kind of far-reaching, and sometimes where you think there might not be support, there is. But this is not something that should be taken for granted.

Be prepared. Keep these networks going, and be ready to respond when it's needed, because you do have power. You also have power through connections. If you lay the groundwork, those connections beat the highest paid lobbyists. Protect what you have.

Retired Senator Gen Olson (on left) receives the Schurke Friend of Home Education Award from Merryl Schurke (on right).

Chapter Twenty-Seven

Mike Donnelly joins the Home School Legal Defense Association (HSLDA), helps Minnesota's homeschoolers who are in need of legal assistance, and works with MÂCHÉ to bring about favorable legislation for homeschoolers.

Interview (September 27, 2013) with:
Michael Donnelly (HSLDA Attorney)

HSLDA
Mike:

I came to HSLDA in September 2006, and I was privileged to be given the responsibility to handle member affairs in Minnesota. HSLDA helps individual families defend themselves from superintendents and school officials who don't understand the law or who want more than they are allowed under the law.

We help families when they encounter Social Services, investigations related to truancy, or other issues. We've had some pretty serious Social Services investigations in Minnesota. I've seen a few families in Minnesota just be really manhandled by the state authorities. Some have left Minnesota because of this.

HSLDA has helped a number of families in Minnesota. Every year there are always superintendents who are asking for vaccination forms they don't deserve or information before the October 1st deadline. Whenever that kind of stuff happens, HSLDA sends out letters to those superintendents, and emails out to let HSLDA members know, "Hey, this is what happened. So don't let it happen to you." That is one aspect of what we do.

The other aspect of what we do is working with MÂCHÉ and the legislature in Minnesota. Right now, you guys have John Tuma, who is probably one of the best, if not the best, legislative liaisons in the country for homeschoolers, and our job is supporting him in his efforts to advance freedom for homeschooling.

Homeschool Mandate Reduction Bill

Mike:

Legislatively, one of the things I really enjoyed doing in Minnesota was with John Tuma. We started talking in 2008 or 2009 about seeing if we could improve the law. We came up with some ideas, and we worked on drafting the legislation together. Of course, Gen Olson was involved there. She's a great friend of homeschooling, and she was willing to go to bat.

During the economic crisis when the state was looking for any way they could save money, we thought maybe the state would give us more freedom and let us not have to fill out all of this paperwork. The idea was to reduce mandates on the superintendents and get something in return. We called it the "Mandate Reduction Bill."

The two big things were not having to file the annual report and not doing quarterly reports. The superintendents have all of this paperwork, and who wants to file all that? You don't really need all that information anyway, and quarterly reports, that's kind of passé.

Superintendents and others seemed to be okay with the paperwork changes, and we're like "Hmm, okay. Let's keep going with this."

The next year we kept working. The bill didn't make it that year [2010], but then the next year [2011], it made it. So now in Minnesota, homeschoolers without a bachelor's degree no longer have to send in quarterly reports, and that's a good number of homeschoolers.

People are also saved a lot of hassle and don't have to fill out a report yearly. They just have to do one notice of intent, and then they just send in a renewal.

We had a few problems during the transition time with superintendents who misunderstood the law or didn't know that the law had changed. Each year we have a few of those.

The Minnesota fight was a joint effort. We worked together and mostly behind the scenes really. It did not require a lot of brute force, because you have such an effective legislative liaison in John Tuma and a great champion in Gen Olson. Gen is tremendously respected in the Senate and has been involved in education for a long time. When you have those kinds of friends and people working on your behalf, you can get a lot done.

One thing I think is kind of funny is early on John Tuma described to me how superintendents and education people in Minnesota see HSLDA. We had just begun working on the "Mandate Reduction Bill," and he was talking to a superintendent and HSLDA's name came up, and the superintendent said, "Oh, those guys. Those guys who send those hateful, nasty letters to people all of the time?"

It was funny for me to hear that that is how some of the superintendents see HSLDA. And, of course, we do send lawyer letters. They are not nasty letters. They are polite and professional, but a letter from a lawyer can often accomplish a lot. Superintendents don't want to hassle with lawyers, and they don't want to have to get their own lawyers involved. So that ends up solving a lot of problems.

Working with MÂCHÉ
Mike:

I have worked closely with David Watkins and John Tuma. We've had a great working relationship. I so appreciate both of them and their leadership, and I have come to see the MÂCHÉ organization as one of the leading homeschool organizations in the country. I think it is one of the most well-organized, well-led, effective homeschool organizations in the country, and I see a lot of homeschool organizations. There are fifty states plus six territories, and most of them have some kind of association.

I've enjoyed speaking at the MÂCHÉ conferences.

I love coming out to all the different locations. John's Barbecue in Rochester is a top place for me. It's this little hole-in-the-wall place, but I really like barbecue and finding John's Barbecue was great. It's like a diamond in the rough.

Advice

Mike:

Do not weary of well doing, and persist.

The homeschooling approach allows families to be what God intended them to be. For Christian families, homeschooling is the most effective way to fulfill their God-given responsibility to disciple their children in a relationship with God through Jesus Christ.

At the end of the day, you can learn math, science, social studies, and history, but it's not what you know; it's Who you know. Keep homeschooling your kids.

I would say to the next generation, follow God's plan for your life and, no matter what it is, it will be great. Homeschooling is one of those great things that I hope the next generation will continue.

Appendix A
Legal and Legislative Sources

I.

An Act Requiring the Education of All Healthy Children
CHAPTER 197.

Be it enacted by the Legislature of the State of Minnesota:

Section 1. That *every parent, guardian, or other person in the state of Minnesota having control of any child or children between the ages of eight and sixteen years shall be required to send such child . . . to a public school, or private school, taught by a competent instructor, for a period of at least twelve weeks in each year, at least six weeks of which time shall be consecutive* [emphasis added], unless such child or children are excused from such attendance by the board of the school district . . . in which such parent, guardian or person having control resides, upon its being shown to their satisfaction that such parent or guardian was not able, by reason of poverty, to clothe such child properly or that such child's bodily or mental condition has been such as to prevent his attendance at school or application to study for the period required, *or that such child or children are taught at home in such branches of study as are usually taught in the public schools subject to the same examination as other pupils of the district or city* [emphasis added] in which the child resides, or that he has already acquired the ordinary branches required by law, or that there is no school taught within two miles by the nearest traveled road . . .

Any parent, guardian or other person failing to comply with the provisions of this act shall, upon conviction, be deemed guilty of a misdemeanor . . .

It shall be the duty of any school director or president of the board of education to inquire into all cases of neglect of the duty prescribed in this act . . .

An Act Requiring the Education of All Healthy Children. (1885). Minnesota Legislative Reference Library, Session Law Archive, 1885-1886, *available at* https://www.revisor.mn.gov/data/revisor/law/1885/0/1885-197.pdf

II.
Pierce v. Society of Sisters

Under the doctrine of *Meyer v. Nebraska*, 262 U.S. 390, 43 S. Ct. 625, 29 A. L. R. 1146, we think it entirely plain that the Act of 1922 unreasonably interferes with the liberty of parents and guardians to direct the upbringing and education of children [268 U.S. 510, 535] under their control. As often heretofore pointed out, rights guaranteed by the Constitution may not be abridged by legislation which has no reasonable relation to some purpose within the competency of the state. *The fundamental theory of liberty upon which all governments in this Union repose excludes any general power of the state to standardize its children by forcing them to accept instruction from public teachers only. The child is not the mere creature of the state; those who nurture him and direct his destiny have the right, coupled with the high duty, to recognize and prepare him for additional obligations* [emphasis added].

Pierce v. Society of Sisters, 268 U.S. 510, 534-35 (1925), *available at* http://caselaw.lp.findlaw.com/scripts/getcase.pl?court=US&vol=268&invol=510

III.
The State of Tennessee v. John Thomas Scopes

July 21, 1925 - **The Scopes Trial**, formally known as The State of Tennessee v. John Thomas Scopes and **commonly referred to as the Scopes Monkey Trial**, was a famous American legal case in 1925 in which a high school teacher, John Scopes, was accused of violating Tennessee's Butler Act, which made it unlawful to teach human evolution in any state-funded school. The trial was deliberately staged in order to attract publicity to the small town of Dayton, Tennessee, where it was held . . .

Scopes was found guilty and fined $100, but the verdict was overturned on a technicality. The trial served its purpose of drawing intense national publicity, as national reporters flocked to Dayton to cover the big-name lawyers who had agreed to represent each side. William Jennings Bryan, three-time presidential candidate, argued for the prosecution, while Clarence Darrow, the famed defense attorney, spoke for Scopes. The trial publicized the Fundamentalist-Modernist Controversy, which set Modernists, who said evolution was not inconsistent with religion, against Fundamentalists, who said the word of God as revealed in the Bible took priority over all human knowledge. The case was thus seen as both a theological contest and a trial on whether modern science regarding the creation-evolution controversy should be taught in schools.

Scopes Trial. In *Wikipedia*. Retrieved December 23, 2013, from http://en.wikipedia.org/wiki/Scopes_Trial

(Authors' note: We used this concise *Wikipedia* summary for a quick reference. For more scholarly study, please consult the Bluebook citation below.)

See also *Scopes v. State*, 154 Tenn. 105 (1927).

IV.
Prayer and Bible Reading Taken Out of Public Schools

In two landmark decisions, Engel v. Vitale (1962) and Abington School District v. Schempp (1963), the US Supreme Court established what is now the current prohibition on state-sponsored prayer in schools. While the Engel decision held that the promulgation of an official state-school prayer stood in violation of the First Amendment's Establishment Clause (thus overruling the New York Courts' decisions), Abington held that Bible readings and other (state) school-sponsored religious activities were prohibited. Following these two cases came the Court's decision in Lemon v. Kurzman (1971), a ruling that established the Lemon test for religious activities within schools.

The Lemon test states that in order to be constitutional under the Establishment Clause of the First Amendment any practice sponsored within state-run schools (or other public, state sponsored activities) must adhere to the following three criteria:

1. Have a secular purpose;
2. Must neither advance nor inhibit religion; and
3. Must not result in an excessive entanglement between government and religion.

School Prayer. 1963 and after. In *Wikipedia*. Retrieved December 23, 2013, from http://en.wikipedia.org/wiki/School_prayer

(Authors' note: We used this concise *Wikipedia* summary for a quick reference. For more scholarly study, please consult the Bluebook citation below.)

See also *Lemon v. Kurtzman*, 403 U.S. 602 (1971).

V.
Wisconsin v. Yoder

May 15, 1972
Syllabus
Respondents, members of the Old Order Amish religion and the Conservative Amish Mennonite Church, were convicted of violating Wisconsin's compulsory school attendance law (which requires a child's school attendance until age 16) by declining to send their children to public or private school after they had graduated from

the eighth grade. The evidence showed that the Amish provide continuing informal vocational education to their children designed to prepare them for life in the rural Amish community. The evidence also showed that respondents sincerely believed that high school attendance was contrary to the Amish religion and way of life, and that they would endanger their own salvation and that of their children by complying with the law. The State Supreme Court sustained respondents' claim that application of the compulsory school attendance law to them violated their rights under the Free Exercise Clause of the First Amendment, made applicable to the States by the Fourteenth Amendment.

Held:

1. The State's interest in universal education is not totally free from a balancing process when it impinges on other fundamental rights, such as those specifically protected by the Free Exercise Clause of the First Amendment and the traditional interest of parents with respect to the religious upbringing of their children. Pp. 213-215.

2. Respondents have amply supported their claim that enforcement of the compulsory formal education requirement after the eighth grade would gravely endanger if not destroy the free exercise of their religious beliefs. Pp. 215-219

3. Aided by a history of three centuries as an identifiable religious sect and a long history as a successful and self-sufficient segment of American society, the Amish have demonstrated the sincerity of their religious beliefs, the interrelationship of belief with their mode of life, the vital role that belief and daily conduct play in the continuing survival of Old Order Amish communities, and the hazards presented by the State's enforcement of a statute generally valid as to others. Beyond this, they have carried the difficult burden of demonstrating the adequacy of their alternative mode of continuing informal vocational education in terms of the overall interest that the State relies on in support of its program of compulsory high school education. In light of this showing, and weighing the minimal difference between what the State would require and what the Amish already accept, it was incumbent on

the State to show with more particularity how its admittedly strong interest in compulsory education would be adversely affected by granting an exemption to the Amish. Pp. 212-29, 234-236.

4. *The State's claim that it is empowered, as parens patriae, to extend the benefit of secondary education to children regardless of the wishes of their parents cannot be sustained against a free exercise claim of the nature revealed by this record, for the Amish have introduced convincing evidence that accommodating their religious objections by forgoing one or two additional years of compulsory education will not impair the physical or mental health of the child, or result in an inability to be self-supporting or to discharge the duties and responsibilities of citizenship, or in any other way materially detract from the welfare of society* [emphasis added]. Pp. 229-234.

49 Wis.2d 430, 182 N.W.2d 539, affirmed.

BURGER, C.J., delivered the opinion of the Court, in which BRENNAN, STEWART, WHITE, MARSHALL, and BLACKMUN, JJ., joined. STEWART, J., filed a concurring opinion, in which BRENNAN, J., joined, post, p. 237. WHITE, J., filed a concurring opinion, in which BRENNAN and STEWART, JJ., joined, post, p. 237. DOUGLAS, J., filed an opinion dissenting in part, post, p. 241. POWELL and REHNQUIST, JJ., took no part in the consideration or decision of the case.

Wisconsin v. Yoder, 406 U.S. 205, 205-7 (1972), *available at* http://www.law.cornell.edu/supremecourt/text/406/205

VI.
State of Minnesota vs. Donald and Kathleen Budke: Order on Appeal

November 1, 1983
This is an appeal from the August 18 and September 14, 1982, orders of The Honorable Sigwel Wood, Otter Tail County Court, finding

Donald and Kathleen Budke in violation of the State's compulsory education law, Minn. Stat. 120.10. We reverse. *State v. Budke*, 1 (Minn. Ct. App. 2001).

[The] appellants believe, in essence, that to send a child to a system of education which does not center around the Bible and which does not teach faith in Jesus Christ, is to endanger the eternal destiny of that child and to bring God's judgment upon oneself as well. *Id.* at 4 n.2.

It is the holding of this Court, that [the] Appellants' belief grows out of deeply held religious convictions, which are entitled to the protection of the First Amendment, as applied to states by the Fourteenth Amendment. *Id.* at 5.

The public policy behind a state's interest in education is to insure the education necessary to prepare citizens to participate intelligently and effectively in the open political system and to prepare individuals to be self-reliant and self-sufficient participants in society [emphasis added]. *Id.* at 6.

There is also uncontradicted testimony by experts in education that Mrs. Budke is doing an effective job and that [the] Appellants' home school completely fulfills the State's interest in preparing children for citizenship and productive occupations, that is, the children are receiving a good education. *Id.* at 7.

Quality education is evidence of a good teacher, as well as evidence that the State's interest in education is being met [emphasis added]. *Id.* at 7.

In essence, Appellants have taken the only course of action available that is consistent with their religious convictions and with their children's need for a good education. The State's interest in requiring a baccalaureate degree, in light of evidence that quality teaching is being provided, is not sufficient to overbalance the burden placed on their free exercise interest. *Id.* at 8.

Budke Appellate Panel—State of Minnesota—County of Otter Tail—In District Court Seventh Judicial District. Original Document (Authors' note: The original document cited above is an unpublished case and not available in print or online. Consult *State v. Newstrom* for further information.)

See also *State v. Budke*, 371 N.W.2d 533 (Minn. 1985).

VII.
State of Minnesota v. Jeanne Newstrom

July 19, 1985

Minn. Stat. 120.10, subd. 2 (1984), which defines "school" in part as one in which the curriculum is taught by teachers whose qualifications are "essentially equivalent" to those of public school teachers, is unconstitutionally vague, under the United States Constitution, amendment XIV and the Minnesota Constitution, art. 1, S 7, for purposes of imposing criminal penalties on persons charged with violating the compulsory school attendance law. Reversed. *State v. Newstrom*, 371 N.W.2d 525, 526 (Minn. 1985).

In August, 1981, [ISD 316 Superintendent] Maertens advised Jeanne Newstrom by letter that her school was being denied recognition and that she must send the children full time to the public school . . . . On October 8, 1982, Maertens filed a complaint against Jeanne Newstrom, charging her with a misdemeanor for willful noncompliance with section 120.12, subd. 3, the compulsory attendance law, because her home school did not comply with Minn. Stat. S 120.10, subd. 2 (1984) in that she lacked the formal education training required of teachers under that statute. *Id.*at 526.

The State did not claim that Jeanne Newstrom was not a good teacher or that her school was not a school in the usual sense of the word. Rather, the State argued that her lack of formal educational training automatically demonstrated that her qualifications were not essentially equivalent to those required of a public school teacher. *Id.*at 527.

Jeanne Newstrom gave testimony regarding the structure of her school and the nature of its curriculum. She also sought to demonstrate that her children had performed successfully on standardized national tests. The trial court would not admit this evidence. *Id.*at 527.

The trial court took the position that Jeanne Newstrom's qualifications were to be determined solely on the basis of her educational training and disallowed evidence bearing upon how she taught, test results which indicated how well she taught, her life experiences as relevant to her educational knowledge, her philosophy of education, her reasons for teaching her children at home, and the effectiveness of her children's home schooling. The court also excluded from evidence an exhibit tending to show the Newstroms' good faith attempts to prove to Maertens that the Newstrom Family School was a bonafide school. *Id.*at 527.

During final argument, Jeanne Newstrom's attorney attempted to argue that experience, knowledge, and performance were relevant to the issue of "essential equivalence." He also sought to argue that Jeanne Newstrom should be acquitted because the teacher requirements in section 120.10, subd. 2, were unclear. In each instance, the trial court sustained objections to this line of argument. *Id.*at 527.

The jury found Jeanne Newstrom guilty and the trial court sentenced her to serve 30 days in jail or to pay a $300 fine and a $30 surcharge. On appeal, the conviction was affirmed by a three-judge district court panel. We [the Supreme Court] granted discretionary review. *Id.*at 527.

[A] statute which provides, as does section 120.10, the basis of a criminal prosecution, must meet due process standards of definiteness under both the United States Constitution and the Minnesota Constitution. Persons of common intelligence must not be left to guess at the meaning of a statute nor differ as to its application. *Id.*at 528.

The trial courts in Minnesota have arrived at directly conflicting interpretations of the statute. The lower courts in this case and the trial court in *State v. Budke*, filed today, concluded that "essentially equivalent" means "the same as" and thus a parent must have at least a baccalaureate degree to be legally entitled to teach his or her child at home. Other Minnesota trial courts have read the requirements in section 120.10, subdivision 2, differently. *Id.*at 528.

For example . . . Hennepin County District Court File No.89134 (decided March 2, 1978), the trial court exonerated parents who were educating their child at home, accepting a "proof of qualifications is in the results" argument. The court explained:

> The Court is more concerned with the ability of the teachers to instruct than with the extent to which they have themselves been formally instructed. All indications are that the child has been well instructed in the compulsory areas required by Minnesota law as well as in numerous other areas which may well serve her through the years. *Id.*at 528.

Since the trial court judges in this state cannot agree upon a reading of section 120.10, subdivision 2, it is reasonable to conclude that laypersons would have even greater difficulty in interpreting it. *Id.*at 529.

[The] circumstances under which a child is educated can and do impart to children social messages of their claims to equality and self-respect which "may affect their hearts and minds in a way unlikely ever to be undone." *Brown*, 347 U.S. at 494. *Id.*at 532.

We do not mean to suggest that under no circumstances could parents' interest in directing their child's education ever outweigh the state's interest in enforcing its compulsory attendance laws or other regulations, or that "home" schooling is not an option that the legislature could or should make more available to children and their parents under certain conditions. *Id.*at 532.

Since Jeanne Newstrom's conviction was based solely upon alleged violations of an unconstitutional statute, that conviction must be reversed. Because our ruling on this issue is dispositive, we need not reach the other issues raised in this appeal.
Reversed. *Id.*at 533.

State v. Newstrom, 371 N.W.2d 525, 526 (Minn. 1985), *available at* http://law.justia.com/cases/minnesota/supreme-court/1985/co-83-1325-2.html

VIII.
Senate File number 1696 a bill for an act relating to education; revising Minnesota Statutes 1985 Supplement, section 120.10.

November 15, 1985
Senators Gen Olson, Jude, Waldorf and Anderson introduce Senate File number 1696 a bill for an act relating to education; revising Minnesota Statutes 1985 Supplement, section 120.10. It is referred to the Committee on Education.
"The legislature finds that it is the right and responsibility of parents to provide a basic education for their children. The need for their basic education is to prepare children to participate effectively and intelligently as citizens and to be self-reliant and self-sufficient members of society.

By this act, the legislature intends to allow parents to exercise this right and responsibility from among a broad range of educational alternatives. At the same time, the legislature intends not to infringe on the primary rights of parents to raise and to teach their children or on the religious beliefs and practices of parents and their children, and of religious organizations." (lines 8-20 S.F. no.1696)
[This bill did not pass.]

S.1096, 1984 Leg. (Minn. 1985).

IX. a.
Compulsory School Attendance Task Force Minutes

June 26, 1986
Commissioner [Ruth] Randall convened the first meeting of the Compulsory Attendance Task Force at 9:00 a.m. The Commissioner welcomed all of the members and briefly reviewed the background of the 1986 enabling legislation which created the Task Force.
Commissioner Randall asked each Task Force member to introduce themselves . . .
The members are as follows:
Bethany Newhouse (Home Education)
Roger Schurke (Home Educators Association)
Dr. William P. Cooney (Parent of a Private School Pupil)
Brother William Rhody (Representative of a Private School Accrediting Association)
Dr. Ed Johnson, Jr. (Representative of a Private Sectarian School)
Patricia Schaefer (Representative of a Private Nonsectarian School)
Charles Lemke (Parent of a Public School Pupil)
Maria Castro Rocha (Public School Teacher)
Dr. Lewis Finch (Public School Administrator)
Marjorie Johnson (Representative of the State Board of Education)
Roberta Margo (Representative of the Board of Teaching)
Dr. Ruth E Randall (The Commissioner of Education)

Upon completion of the introductions, Commissioner Randall welcomed individuals who were attending the meeting as observers and extended greetings to the Task Force members from the authors of the legislation, Senator Jim Pehler, Senator Gen Olson, and Representative Allen Quist . . .

Commissioner Randall asked Mr. Loritz to review in detail the enabling legislation. He explained the background of the legislation, including the 1985 Minnesota Supreme Court decision, State vs. Newstrom which declared that the provision in the current Compulsory Attendance Statute, M.S. 120.10, Subd. 1, "Essentially equivalent teacher," was too vague and that an individual should not be subjected to possible criminal prosecution on the basis of such a vague clause. The court decision did not affect any other provision of the Compulsory Attendance Law or its enforcement. The central issue was the definition of what constitutes a teacher for the purposes of compulsory school attendance.

Mr. Loritz pointed out several new sections of legislation which were enacted in 1986, and will remain in effect until June 30, of 1988. These sections were intended to provide guidance until the Legislature had an opportunity to review the findings of this Task Force . . . . Mr. Loritz reviewed the first Minnesota Compulsory Attendance Statute, enacted in 1885, which still exists today with only slight modification as the current Compulsory Attendance Statute . . .

The Task Force voted unanimously to elect Commissioner Randall Chairperson . . . Mr. Loritz would be her alternate . . . . It was agreed that each member could have one formal alternate . . .

Roger Schurke indicated that one of the areas that needed to be discussed thoroughly was the issue of whether or not education was the right of the parent and that right as it relates to the responsibility of the school . . .

Brother William Rhody asked if there was a way that we could test our agreement on any of the issues. He indicated it would be extremely beneficial if we could get a list of the items we agreed upon so that we could spend the balance of our time talking about those fundamental issues where disagreement exists. Brother Rhody indicated that we must clarify and be precise on our terms concerning compulsory "attendance" and compulsory "education." . . .

Roger Schurke indicated that this entire issue really centered around the definition of a "school." He expressed his hope that the Task Force could arrive at a precise definition.

Lew Finch suggested that the task force attempt to define the issues and then check for agreement on those issues. For example, is the primary responsibility for education that of the parent? . . .

Brother Rhody indicated that the task force should attempt to generate a list of "I believe" statements . . . [which] could be brought to future meetings for discussion.

Lew Finch indicated that the court case really only dealt with the "essentially equivalent teacher" issue. He further indicated that perhaps since that was the only issue in question that the Task Force may want to focus its efforts on that issue.

Roger Schurke indicated that from his understanding of the legislation, that the issue of "essentially equivalent teacher" was not the only issue that needed to be discussed by the Task Force.

Brother William Rhody suggested that each Task Force member generate a list of "I believe statements" and have them sent to the Task Force staff to be mailed to all members prior to the next meeting . . . the August 7 meeting would then provide an opportunity to discuss the "I believe statements" and begin to move towards the "we agree statements."

Roberta Margo asked whether or not Task Force members could submit ideas or background statements on various issues to other members . . .

Maria Castro Rocha moved and Marge Johnson seconded that the Task Force members should submit their "I believe statements" by July 24, 1986, and also any background materials including a one page summary. The motion passed unanimously....

Commissioner Randall indicated that it would seem appropriate to spend the remaining time at this first meeting in clarifying the issues listed in the legislation. The Commissioner indicated that the Task Force could begin with the first issue "Standards for Pupil Performance." . . . The following issues were raised: Which tests? . . . Would only tests be used? . . . Who will determine the standards? . . . What is the least restrictive method to achieve the standards? . . . What are the issues about teaching to the test? . . . Are the expectations (outcomes) clear for student achievement? Who will define them—the state, the school, the parents?

Compulsory Attendance Task Force with the Minnesota Education Commissioner, 26 June 1986 (Minn. 1986). Original Document.

IX. b.

August 7, 1986

The task force continued clarifying the various issues related to the compulsory attendance law. The following is an outline of the discussion which occurred:

Data About Pupil Achievement in Various Types of Schools . . .

Alternative Ways to Comply with the Definition of a School . . .

Accreditation . . .

Correspondence programs . . .

Association with a Church or Religious Organization . . .

Supervision by Teachers . . .

Teacher Qualifications in Various Types of Schools, Including Licensure and Ways to Determine Teacher Effectiveness . . .

Reporting Requirements . . .

Methods of Enforcement . . .

Penalties for Noncompliance . . .

The following "I Believe Statements" were completed by the Task Force:

The best interest of the State is served by a citizenry equipped to exercise maximum independent action with an awareness of a concern for the common welfare of the society [emphasis added].

I believe that all educators whether public or private, including home-schools, must work in a cooperative and mutually beneficial manner to achieve the common goal they share which is the education of children.

I believe it is a parent's primary right and responsibility to determine the means by which his or her child will receive an education [emphasis added].

Compulsory Attendance Task Force with the Minnesota Education Commissioner, 7 August 1986 (Minn. 1986). Original Document.

IX. c.

November 6, 1986

Three task force members handed out materials for other members to study.

Dr. Finch submitted a one page summary of a recent court decision upholding a North Dakota Supreme Court ruling that had affirmed the conviction of four families for violating state compulsory school attendance laws. Also, he shared a memo from Janet Davenport, an employee of Anoka Hennepin School District, which outlined a complaint from a noncustodial parent about the home-educating of his son in that district.

Brother William Rhody submitted copies of the Wisconsin law (passed in 1983) that governs private and public schools in that state.

Roger Schurke distributed copies of "Home School Statute Chart of the 50 States," a summary of state laws relating to home schools prepared by Christopher J. Klicka, J.D., Executive Director of the Home School Legal Defense Association. Brief discussion occurred regarding these materials.

Compulsory Attendance Task Force with the Minnesota Education Commissioner, 6 November 1986 (Minn. 1986). Original Document.

IX. d.

December 16, 1986

Mickey Cooney distributed copies of a proposal from Dr. William Cooney relating to teacher qualifications and assessment of student performance. Concluding that two issues now divide the task force— qualifications of those providing education and assessment of student performance—Dr. Cooney outlined the nature of an "Advisory Board of Nonpublic (Private) Education." As with Brother William Rhody's proposal, Dr. Cooney's nonpublic board would be limited to two functions: approval of accrediting agencies and approval of standardized tests.

Roger Schurke then distributed copies of a proposed revision of current law relating to compulsory school attendance. This included proposals relating to all the major elements of a new law. It was summarized by Mr. Schurke, and the group compared his recommendations with those of alternative proposals [emphasis added].

After a short recess from 10:39 to 10:52, the task force used the remaining time to discuss the "Outline of a Compulsory Education Law" that staff had prepared for this meeting. Most of the discussion centered on "Qualifications of Instructor" and the various options listed under that heading. After quickly agreeing that the first three options should be included, considerable time was devoted to the nature of a private education board, or an advisory group controlled by representatives of nonpublic education that would perform certain functions. The central issue dividing task force members, it appeared, was the extent of duties to give this nonpublic education entity: representatives from public school groups wanted it restricted to approving accrediting agencies, while those from the nonpublic sector urged that it should also approve a list of tests from which their school officials could select particular instruments to assess students.

During this discussion, **Bethany Newhouse** distributed copies of a comparison of recommendations from the various sources which the task force has been reviewing. This working document was used by the task force as they attempted to contrast the various proposals, especially those relating to teacher qualifications and student assessment.

As the meeting neared its end, the task force decided to add another meeting to its January schedule.

Compulsory Attendance Task Force with the Minnesota Education Commissioner, 16 December 1986 (Minn. 1986). Original Document.

X.
The Compulsory Attendance Task Force Submits an Outline for a Compulsory Education Law

Minnesota Department of Education [Letterhead]
January 12, 1987

Minnesota Senate and House of Representatives
State Capitol
Saint Paul, Minnesota 55155

Members of Senate and House Education Committees:

This communication is to submit to you the outline for a compulsory education law. The outline was developed by the task force which you directed in Chapter 472, 1986 Session Law.

The task force first met in June, 1986, and held a final meeting on January 12, 1987. Members of the task force contributed 41.5 hours of time in 14 meetings over the past 7 months.

Task force members contributed considerable time prior to each meeting in studying compulsory education issues. During our meetings, we learned to know one another through sharing our deep convictions and strong beliefs.

This outline of a compulsory education law could become the basis for legislation. We are pleased that we could achieve consensus on all of the elements within the outline. We look forward to working with you in whatever ways could be helpful to you.

Sincerely,
Compulsory School Attendance Task Force

Compulsory School Attendance Task Force: Letter to S. and H. Comm. on Education, 1986 Leg. (Minn. 1987). Original Document.

XI.
House Research Bill Summary on Compulsory Attendance

February 23, 1987
H.F. 432

Subject: Compulsory Attendance
Authors: McEachern, K. Nelson, Olsen, Kostohryz, Kelso
Committee: Education

...

Section 9.

Section 120.10, subd. 1: specifies ages and school terms for compulsory attendance

Section 120.10, subd. 2: defines a school for purposes of compulsory attendance

Section 120.10, subd. 2a: requires a parent teaching a child at home to report the name, age and address of the child to the local superintendent by October 1 of each year (enacted in 1986)

Section 120.10, subd. 2b: states that civil or criminal proceedings will not be brought against a parent teaching a child at home in compliance with subdivision 2. (enacted in 1986)

Section 120.12: specifies the enforcement procedures for compulsory attendance violations

H.R. Doc. Summary of H.F. 432, 1986 Leg. (Minn. 1987).

XII.
Minnesota House of Representatives House Education Committee Meeting

Minnesota House of Representatives [Letterhead]
House Education Committee
Rep. Bob McEachern, Chair
Wednesday, February 25, 1987
8:00 a.m.
Room 5, State Office Building
AGENDA

I. Call to Order
II. Roll Call

III. Approval of Minutes: February 18, 1987

IV. H.F. 432 (McEachern) Modifying certain provisions of the compulsory attendance laws; establishing new compulsory attendance requirements.

    A. Historical Overview
       Marsha Gronseth, Legal Counsel

    B. Recommendations from the Compulsory School Attendance Task Force
       Dr. Ruth Randall, Commissioner of Education
       Dr. Lew Finch, Superintendent, Anoka Public Schools
       Brother William Rhody, MN Nonpublic School Accrediting Association

    C. Summary of H.F. 432
       Representative Bob McEachern
       Public Testimony:
            Wayne Olhoft, Education Freedom Fund
            Jim Hamstra
            Cathy Lytle
            Ms. Solveig Swanson
            Robert Newhouse, Director, TEACH
            Rose Hermodson, MN Federation of Teachers
            Ken Bressin, MN Education Association
            Carl Johnson, MN School Boards Association

V. Future Meetings: Education Finance Division, Today, 2:00 P.M., 300N

VI. Adjournment

H.R. Education Committee Meeting Agenda, 1986 Leg. (Minn. 1987). Original Document.

XIII.
Senate Education Committee Passes H.F. 432

Minnesota Department of Education [Letterhead]
MEMORANDUM

TO: Compulsory Education Task Force Members
FROM: Barry Sullivan
DATE: April 15, 1987
SUBJECT: Compulsory Education Bill

The Senate Education Committee today passed H.F. 432, the house-passed version of your recommendations.

After testimony from representatives of the task force—Dr. Lew Finch, Brother William Rhody, and Roger Schurke—followed by numerous questions and proposed amendments, the bill was sent to the floor on a vote of 16-3. A few amendments were adopted. I have penciled in the amendments on the attached copy of H.F. 432. . . .

I don't believe these changes are substantive . . . . The next step is floor action in the Senate. Though the wide vote margin should bode well, political support changes rapidly—as shown by comparing committee action today with a few weeks ago when this same group voted 13-5 to essentially gut the bill by adopting the major amendment I sent to you earlier.

Let me know if you have any questions. I'll contact you when action occurs on the Senate floor.

Sullivan, B. (1987, April 15). Minnesota Department of Education memorandum to the Compulsory Education Task Force [Memorandum]. Original Document.

XIV.
The Compulsory Attendance Bill Becomes Law

120.101 Compulsory Instruction

Subd. 7. **Requirements for instructors**. A person who is providing instruction to a child must meet at least one of the following requirements:

  (1) hold a valid Minnesota teaching license in the field and for the grade level taught;

(2) be directly supervised by a person holding a valid Minnesota teaching license;

(3) successfully complete a teacher competency examination;

(4) provide instruction in a school that is accredited by an accrediting agency, recognized according to section 123.935, subdivision 7, or recognized by the state board of education;

(5) hold a baccalaureate degree; or

(6) be the parent of a child who is assessed according to the procedures in subdivision 8.

Any person providing instruction in a public school must meet the requirements of clause (1).

Subd. 8. **Assessment of performance**. (a) Each year the performance of every child who is not enrolled in a public school must be assessed using a nationally norm-referenced standardized achievement examination. The superintendent of the district in which the child receives instruction and the person in charge of the child's instruction must agree about the specific examination to be used and the administration and location of the examination.

(b) To the extent the examination in paragraph (a) does not provide assessment in all of the subject areas in subdivision 6, the parent must assess the child's performance in the applicable subject area. This requirement applies only to a parent who provides instruction and does not meet the requirements of subdivision 7, clause (1), (2), or (3).

(c) If the results of the assessments in paragraphs (a) and (b) indicate that the child's performance on the total battery score is at or below the 30th percentile or one grade level below the performance level for children of the same age, the parent shall obtain additional evaluation of the child's abilities and performance for the purpose of determining whether the child has learning problems.

Minn. Stat. § 120.101 (1987), *available at* https://www.revisor.mn.gov/data/revisor/statute/1987/1987-120.pdf

XV.
Minnesota Home Schoolers Defeat
Attempts at More Regulation

ST. PAUL, MINNESOTA—Hundreds of Minnesota home school families converged on the Senate Education Committee yesterday, March 21, 2001, and successfully derailed an attempt by the legislature to increase home school regulations in the state.

According to current state law, parents are already required to submit annual notices of intent, meet certain teacher qualifications or file quarterly reports, and administer annual standardized tests to their children.

Under one portion of Senate Bill 866, home schooling parents who are already providing effective home education, would have been required to prove they have a high school diploma. But the committee heard convincing testimony that studies on home schooling reveal that parents who have not completed high school are more than capable of teaching their own children effectively through high school.

Because home schoolers demonstrated their opposition to this provision in such numbers, the committee defeated that part of the bill unanimously.

Christopher Klicka, senior counsel with the Home School Legal Defense Association, traveled to Minnesota to support the work of state home school leaders fighting the bill.

"Minnesota home schoolers provided an incredible response. We had a definite sense that the committee was impressed with how many people showed up to resist this attack on parental rights and home school freedom," Klicka said.

Most of the home schoolers in attendance could not fit in the committee room. They were forced to listen to the testimony on a public address system. Although vocal responses were not allowed in the committee room, committee members could hear the cheering at key points in the testimony from home school families packed in the hallways and adjacent rooms.

Minnesota law now dictates that parents administer standardized tests to their children, but under S.B. 866 state regulation would increase tremendously by requiring parents to annually submit standardized test scores to their local superintendents. This part of the bill was defeated 23-7.

Minnesota already has some of the most burdensome regulations for home schoolers, Klicka said. "Minnesota home schoolers and their leaders are doing a great job. If anything, Minnesota ought to commend its home schoolers by reducing the regulations, not by trying to make things tougher on these families."

The Associate Press ran a wire story covering yesterday's Senate Education Committee hearing. It was published at http://www.pioneerplanet.com and http://www.startribune.com/. The Star Tribune and Pioneer Press are published in Minneapolis-St. Paul.

Jefferson, R. (2001, March 22). Minnesota home schoolers defeat attempts at more regulation [HSLDA media release]. Retrieved December 23, 2013, from http://www.hslda.org/docs/news/hslda/200103220.asp

XVI.
Rodney LeVake vs. Independent School District 656

Filed May 8, 2001
Affirmed
Foley, Judge
Rice County District Court
File No. CX-99-793

Appellant, a high school science teacher, challenges the district court's summary judgment in favor of respondent's school district, superintendent, principal, and curriculum director. Appellant argues that he presented a genuine issue of material fact precluding summary judgment on the issue of whether respondents violated his rights of free exercise of religion, free speech, and due process by reassigning him to teach a different class after discovering that appellant wanted to teach criticisms of evolution. Appellant also argues that the district court erred by excluding a portion of his deposition testimony as hearsay and considering a videotaped interview of appellant. Because appellant refused to teach his assigned class in the manner prescribed by the established curriculum, we conclude that he did not present any genuine issue of material fact, and we affirm.

LeVake v. Independent School District # 656, 625 N.W.2d 502, 504-5 (Minn. Ct. App. 2001), *available at* http://mn.gov/lawlib/archive/ctappub/0105/c8001613.htm

XVII.
The Mandate Reduction Bill

February 3, 2011, "Home Schools Mandates and Reporting Requirements Reduction" bill introduced and read in the House.
House File 355 was referred to the Education Reform Committee.
February 24, 2011, the House Education Reform Committee recommends "to pass" and refers the bill to the Education Finance Committee.
March 7, 2011, at the 3rd reading the S.F. 69 Mandate Reduction bill is passed in the Senate and sent to the House. At its first reading in the House it is sent to the Education Finance Committee.
July 20, 2011, **The "Home Schools Mandates and Reporting Requirements Reduction" is passed in House Bill 26.**

Senate Sponsors
Senators Gen Olson, Stumpf, Nienow, Wolf, and Chamberlain

House Sponsors
Kiffmeyer, Erickson, Myhra, Drazkowski, Woodard, B. Petersen, Kiel, Abeler, Wardlow, Barrett, Lohmer, and Dettmer

Summary:
If passed, these bills would substantially reduce reporting requirements for homeschool families and would thus extend homeschool freedom in Minnesota. The bill would make the following changes:
1) Limit annual notification reporting to one-time reporting when a family starts homeschooling, or when they move; subsequent renewals would be a simple letter of "intent to continue" with any updated information. 2) Give students the option to take a nationally recognized college entrance exam in lieu of a standardized achievement test; 3) Eliminate the requirement that parents obtain additional evaluation of a student's abilities should the student scores below the 30th percentile; 4) Eliminates annual visit by superintendent; 5) Eliminate the requirement that parents submit an annual instructional calendar; 6) Eliminate the requirement that parents without certain qualifications submit quarterly reports; 7) Require parents to simply maintain (vs. make available) documentation that the student is being taught the required subjects; 8) Allow a parent to certify that a student is presently engaged in home education for the purposes of taking home-classroom driver training; 9) Allow the person in charge of providing instruction in a homeschool to issue an employment certificate; 10) Limit immunization reporting requirements to only the first year of homeschooling and the 7th grade year.

Homeschool Legal Defense Association. (2011). Senate File 69/ House File 355: Home schools mandates and reporting requirements reduction [Summary and status report of bills]. Retrieved December 19, 2013, from http://www.hslda.org/cms/index.php?q=bill/senate-file-69house-file-355-home-schools-mandates-and-reporting-requirements-reduction-0

Appendix B
Other Sources

I.
Michael Farris: Commenting on Drs. Dobson and Moores' Contribution to the Homeschooling Movement

Dr. Michael Farris—"Whenever I am asked what was the catalyst of the modern Christian homeschooling movement, I reply without hesitation—this movement arose when **Dr. James Dobson did his early broadcasts with Dr. Raymond Moore** exposing hundreds of thousands of moms and dads to an absolutely new idea about raising and educating children . . . Dr. James Dobson dared to come onto the radio and say—"God has something to say to you in every part of your life—and this is without exception" . . . The political defense of homeschooling was predicated on a belief that it was OK to be involved in politics and be a Christian . . . Dr. Dobson's willingness to talk about an idea that was so new, so untested in the modern age, so little known, is a credit both to his courage—and I believe even more—a confirmation that he listens to God."

Daly, J. (2009). Two tributes to Dr. James Dobson. Focus on the Family: DalyFocus. Retrieved December 13, 2013, from http://community.focusonthefamily.com/b/jim-daly/archive/2009/10/05/two-tributes-to-dr-james-dobson.aspx

II.
National Commission on Excellence in Education Study

April - We report to the American people that while we can take justifiable pride in what our schools and colleges have historically accomplished and contributed to the United States and the well-being of its people, the educational foundations of our society are presently being eroded by a rising tide of mediocrity that threatens our very future as a national and a people.

National Commission on Excellence in Education. (1983, April). A nation at risk: The imperative for educational reform. A report to the Nation and the Secretary of Education, United States Department of Education [Report]. Retrieved December 17, 2013, from http://datacenter.spps.org/uploads/sotw_a_nation_at_risk_1983.pdf

III.
Remembering the Reason—Renewing the Vision
A Short History of MÂCHÉ
by Merryl Schurke

The Lord brought the Schurke and Coleman families together in the fall of 1983. The previous year, Roger Schurke had met and worked with Michael Farris in Olympia, Washington, a time when the Home School Legal Defense Association was born. The Schurkes had already been homeschooling for five years. Roger's work as an attorney with Mike gave him insight into how to start and maintain an organization.

Upon returning to Minnesota, Roger called pastors and others he knew to find out if there was a state homeschool organization. Many he spoke with referred him to Jim Coleman. Jim and Pam Coleman were meeting with a group that had scientologists among its leadership. Jim, Roger, Pam and Merryl discussed this dilemma and decided that, since most homeschoolers at that time were Christians, Minnesota should have a homeschool organization with Christian leadership. For several weeks, this matter was committed to prayer. It was soon agreed that the Minnesota Association of Christian Home Educators (MÂCHÉ) should hold its organizational meeting. Approximately 50 people attended this meeting in November of

1983 at the Powderhorn Park building in south Minneapolis. Among the attendees were many who continue to homeschool and remain involved with MÂCHÉ.

A decision was made that the board members would be homeschooling Christian couples. The initial member list was kept in the Coleman basement in a container which was originally a cigar box. That list has since grown to over 3,000 and is now kept in a computer in the MÂCHÉ office.

The first MÂCHÉ conference was held at Faith Academy in Fridley with about 300 people in attendance. There were no exhibitors or suppliers, just speakers. The Coleman and Schurke families did all of the mailings by hand and furnished the coffee, cups, napkins and donuts for the first three or four conferences until growth made this impossible. Subsequent conferences were held at Grace Church of Edina, the Edina Community Center, Way of the Cross Church, Crystal Evangelical Free Church, and Bloomington Assembly of God Church.

In 1996 organizational growth and interest made it necessary to begin convening the annual conference at the St. Paul Civic Center which was later named St. Paul RiverCentre. Subsequent conferences have also been held in Rochester and Duluth convention centers. This annual event with an attendance consistently over 5,000 people includes 90+ workshops, 110+ exhibitors, opportunities for mingling with veteran homeschooling parents and Support Group leaders, and plenty of options for food and fellowship.

In 1986, MÂCHÉ, with the help of the Lord and other interested organizations and people, was able to pack the chambers of the Minnesota Legislature with homeschooling families, making a very favorable impression upon the state leaders. Over the years MÂCHÉ has continued to be used of the Lord to take the lead at the Legislature when parents' educational rights and freedoms have been jeopardized.

In the order in which they served, these are the couples who have been board members since MÂCHÉ's inception:

Jim and Pam Coleman
Roger and Merryl Schurke
Jim and Laurie Voeller
Bob and Bethany Newhouse
Chuck and Bobbi Scholander
Dick and Bev Johnson
Pete and Marcia Smith
Carl and Carla Biederman
John and Lynne Cooke
Jerry and Pam von Gohren
Dean and Ruth Lindstrom
Mac and Karen Bryant
Terry and Marcia Van Denburg
David and Linda Watkins
John and Wendy Tuma
Chris and Donna Johnson
Jim and Ruth Brinker
Jim and Julie Walter
Kion and Eileen Hoffman

The current board is comprised of Jim and Ruth Brinker, Kion and Eileen Hoffman, John and Wendy Tuma, and Jim and Julie Walter.

Schurke, M. (2013). Remembering the reason - Renewing the vision: A short history of MÂCHÉ. MÂCHÉ Member's Handbook, 2014, v-vi.

Appendix C
Minnesota Homeschool Support Groups

1982 - Minnetonka Home Education Association (MHEA)

1983 - Rochester Area Association of Christian Home Educators (RAACHE)

1986 - Home Educators and Youth (HEY) Hibbing, Virginia, and St. Louis County, MN

1987 - East Side Christian Home Educators (ESCHEL) Oakdale, MN

Home Educated Youth (HEY) Central MN

Wabasha Area Christian Home Educators (WASHE)

Willmar Area Scholars at Home, Inc. (WASH)

1989 - Plymouth-Wayzata Homeschool Group

Scott County Home Educators (SCHE) Scott, Dakota, and Rice Counties, MN

1990 - Minnehaha Christian Homeschool Co-op South Metro Area, MN

1993 - Anchor Homeschool Group Andover, MN

1994 - Christian Homeschools of Stillwater (CHS)

Resources and Encouragement for Area Christian Homeschoolers (REACH) Moorhead, MN and Fargo, ND

1995 - Montevideo Area Teachers of Children at Home (MATCH)

1997 - Families Embracing Elements of Teaching (FEET) Wright and Sherburne Counties, MN

1998 - Pioneers Grand Rapids, MN

1999 - Kindred Spirits Homeschool Co-op Watertown, MN

Planet Homeschool Minneapolis, MN

2000 - Christ Community Homeschoolers Rochester, MN

2003 - Mankato Area Home Educators (MAHE)

2004 - Catholic Homeschool Alliance Rejoicing in Southwestern Minnesota (CHARISM)

2005 - All Saints Homeschools (ASH) Dakota County, MN

2005 - Bemidji Home School Association (BAHA)

2006 - Hastings Encouragers Dedicated to Godly Education (HEDGE)

2008 - Building Relationships And Networking Homeschoolers (BRANCH) Becker, MN

2012 - Wings of Grace West Metro-Eden Prairie, MN

2013 - Simply Natural Homeschool Co-op New Prague, MN

History Unit Study Guide
by BriAnn Beck

Directions for Highlighting the Text

As you read, use different colored highlighters to mark the following themes in the interviews:

- References to God working in people's lives
- Reasons families start to homeschool, and the people who influence their choice
- Names and progress of specific court cases or bills

Vocabulary/Spelling List

amendment, appeal, association, attendance, committee, compulsory, court, education, equivalence, essential, freedom, government, house, legal, legislature, organization, precedent, senate, socialization, unconstitutional, vague

Comprehension Questions

The questions are arranged by topic with relevant chapter numbers noted.

Some questions are basic fact recall, and others require higher thinking; if you are working through the study guide as a family, save the easier questions for younger students.

(An answer key is included at the end of the study guide.)

Timeline

1. When was the first Compulsory Education Law in Minnesota written? What did it say about homeschooling?
2. What does "compulsory" mean? What does "Compulsory Education/Attendance" mean?
3. What happened in 1925 and 1963 that caused many Christian parents to begin taking their children out of public schools?

4. How old were your grandparents when these things were happening?
5. When was the Moores' "Focus on the Family" radio interview?
6. What does HSLDA stand for? Who founded it, and when? What does the organization do?
7. What does the First Amendment to the US Constitution say? Explain how this applies to homeschooling.
8. What does "useful precedent" mean?
9. What happened on April 17, 2004, and who proclaimed this date special?

MÂCHÉ's Beginning, Chapters 1-2

10. What does MÂCHÉ stand for? Who started MÂCHÉ? When and why?
11. Why was it important that MÂCHÉ be Christian?
12. What was significant about so many teachers attending the first MÂCHÉ conference?
13. What does Jim Coleman mean by not pushing the baby bird out of the nest? Explain his point in your own words.
14. Is homeschooling easy for your parents? What might they have had to give up?

Newstrom Case, Chapter 5

15. What were the arguments Jeanne Newstrom's lawyer made to show that she should be able to continue to teach her children? Which argument do you think was the best? How did the courts respond?
16. What do you think "essentially equivalent" means?
17. Which is more important—that homeschool parents have the same training as public school teachers or that they are good at teaching and their students are learning?
18. What does "appeal" mean?
19. Put the following events from Jeanne Newstrom's legal battle into the correct order:
    lost in district court

accused of a misdemeanor for not sending her children
to public school
appealed to Minnesota Supreme Court
appealed to district court
won in Minnesota Supreme Court
attended pre-trial hearing
lost in county court

Task Force, Chapters 2, 6, 8

20. What is the purpose of standardized testing?
21. What does "unconstitutionally vague" mean?
22. When was the Compulsory School Attendance Task Force created, and why?
23. Was it easy for the task force to agree? If not, why not?
24. What allowed the task force to finally agree and accomplish their goal?
25. What might have happened if Bob Newhouse had not obeyed God and talked to Dr. Finch?
26. Why did Commissioner Randall open the last task force meeting in prayer? Do you think it was effective?
27. What did the Newhouse children bring to every task force meeting to give to the members? How do you think this might have influenced the members? (Optional: Visit one of your legislators or city officials, and write them a thank-you note for their work.)
28. When did the new Compulsory Attendance Law that made homeschooling legal pass? How old were your parents when this happened?

The miracle mentioned in Gen Olson's interview—did you find that miracle in Bob Newhouse's interview?

The Homeschool Law, Chapters 9-11, 13

29. Why were compromise and cooperation necessary in formulating the new law?

30. Explain the following quotes in your own words:
    a) "Never underestimate the power of being right."—Wayne Olhoft
    b) "Eternal vigilance is the price of freedom."—Thomas Jefferson
    c) "We are on the edge of losing our freedom to homeschool every time the legislature is in session."—DuWayne Heppner

Miscellaneous, Chapters 13, 15, 16

31. Why was it hard for early homeschoolers to get curriculum? Do you think it would be hard to figure out your math without solutions?
32. How does the way vendors at MÂCHÉ interact with each other show Christ in them?
33. Why did Maren Stowman's father move the family to the country? What do you think of his decision?
34. Have you or your siblings participated in PSEO or extracurricular school activities?

2001 Hearing and Mandate Reduction, Chapters 16-18, 24-26

35. What was the state trying to require of homeschoolers?
36. Do you think the public schools should get copies of your tests to see how you did?
37. Do you ever help teach your younger siblings? What would you think if the state decided you weren't allowed to do that anymore? Should the state be able to tell you or your parents whether you can teach your own family members?
38. Could you have been as brave as Erin Erpelding? What would you have said to the Senate? (Optional: Use a real or pretend microphone to act it out.)
39. How do you think the behavior of all the homeschool children present might have affected the decision in the legislature that day?
40. What is a mandate?

Wrapping Up

Make a list of all the important people in this book. Include a few words or a sentence telling why they are important. (Optionl: Draw pictures or symbols or use different colors for different topics in their stories.)

What did you learn from your highlighting as you read? (Look especially for similarities between stories.) Write summaries or give oral reports of your findings.

Most of the people interviewed in this book give some of their favorite memories and advice. What are some of your favorite memories? What advice would you give to other homeschoolers?

At the end of the book is a list of homeschool support groups. Look for your group there, and circle it.

Extra Activities

Research and make a flow chart for the process of getting a bill into law. Teach someone else about the process.

Write a paragraph explaining how a committee works within the legislature.

Research *Robert's Rules of Order* (used at the task force meetings), and have a family meeting using them.

Ask your parents why they chose to homeschool you and who influenced them to make that commitment.

Answer Key

1. 1885; homeschooling was legal.
2. Required; parents are required to make sure their children are educated/attend school.

3. Evolution began to be taught in the public schools; prayer and Bible reading were taken out of public schools.
4. Have the children do math problems with the birth dates of parents and grandparents to find their ages at each significant event.
5. 1979
6. Home School Legal Defense Association, founded in 1983, by Farris and Smith; it provides legal advice and assistance to homeschoolers.
7. "Congress shall make no law respecting an establishment of religion, or prohibiting the free exercise thereof," meaning that the government shouldn't keep us from homeschooling if we believe God wants us to.
8. Lawyers in later court cases can show how an earlier case agreed with them.
9. Home Education Day; Governor Pawlenty
10. Minnesota Association of Christian Home Educators, founded by the Schurkes and Colemans in 1983; it provides support for Christian homeschoolers.
11. Your primary support should come from people who share your values.
12. It showed that they were unhappy with the public school from firsthand experience.
13. Prepare your children for the world first before putting them in it.
14. Answers will vary.
15. Her training was "essentially equivalent," and the children were learning; county court declared this irrelevant. It's her constitutional right as a parent to decide how to educate her children; the district court said it's the state's right. The law was too vague to convict her; the Minnesota Supreme Court agreed.
16. Answers will vary.
17. Answers will vary.
18. To ask a higher court to change the decision of a lower court

19. Accused of misdemeanor, pre-trial hearing, lost in county court, appealed to district, lost in district court, appealed to Minnesota Supreme Court, won in Minnesota Supreme Court
20. They help parents see how their children are doing, to make sure they are learning.
21. Normal people have to be able to understand what a law means; otherwise you can't punish them for breaking it.
22. 1986; it was created to determine what should be included in a new Compulsory Attendance Law that would be agreeable to the homeschool, public, and government alike.
23. They had very different values, and some members were prejudiced against others.
24. God helped Bob Newhouse and Lew Finch to break the barriers of prejudice and come to agreement; the commissioner's prayer.
25. Answers will vary.
26. She was following the example of Benjamin Franklin.
27. Homemade bread; answers will vary.
28. April 30, 1987; answers will vary.
29. It had to satisfy everybody from all sides.
30. Answers will vary.
31. They weren't recognized as official schools; answers will vary.
32. They cooperated and helped each other instead of competing.
33. To get away from public school influence; answers will vary.
34. Answers will vary.
35. Report their standardized test results and have a bachelor's degree to teach
36-39. Answers will vary.
40. Something the state tells a local office to do

PSIA information can be obtained at www.ICGtesting.com
inted in the USA
OW05s0622280314

9006BV00002B/2/P